CHEZ L'ARABE

CHEZ L'ARABE

• STORIES •

MIREILLE SILCOFF

This edition published in 2014 by
House of Anansi Press Inc.
110 Spadina Avenue, Suite 801
Toronto, ON, M5V 2K4
Tel. 416-363-4343
Fax 416-363-1017
www.houseofanansi.com

Distributed in Canada by
HarperCollins Canada Ltd.
1995 Markham Road
Scarborough, ON, M1B 5M8
Toll free tel. 1-800-387-0117

House of Anansi Press is committed to protecting our natural
environment. As part of our efforts, the interior of this book is printed
on paper that contains 100% posst-consumer recycled fibres, is acid-free,
and is processed chlorine-free.

18 17 16 15 14   1 2 3 4 5

Library and Archives Canada Cataloguing in Publication

Silcoff, Mireille, 1973–, author
Chez l'arabe : stories / by Mireille Silcoff.

Issued in print and electronic formats.
ISBN 978-1-77089-469-3 (pbk.).—ISBN 978-1-77089-470-9 (html)

I. Title.

PS8637.I353C44 2014   C813'.6   C2014-902778-8
                                              C2014-902779-6

Cover design: Michel Vrana
Text design and typesetting: Alysia Shewchuk

Canada Council   Conseil des Arts   ONTARIO ARTS COUNCIL
for the Arts   du Canada   CONSEIL DES ARTS DE L'ONTARIO

*We acknowledge for their financial support of our publishing program
the Canada Council for the Arts, the Ontario Arts Council, and the
Government of Canada through the Canada Book Fund.*

Printed and bound in Canada

MIX
Paper from
responsible sources
FSC® C004071

For Michael

Saved, rescued, fished-up, half-drowned, out of the deep, dark river, hair shampooed and set. Nobody would know I had ever been in it. Except, of course, that there always remains something

— Jean Rhys, *Good Morning, Midnight*

CONTENTS

CHEZ L'ARABE

THE ATLAS DISPATCHER ALWAYS responded in the same way, as if I didn't call twice a week, the same voice from the same address, asking for exactly the same thing:

"Please send a car with the best and the newest suspension. I have had a very serious head injury."

"Car with good suspension. Ten minutes. Thank you."

It was a kind of politeness. The Atlas drivers were less formal. They knew me by face from before. I was the woman with the long scarves and the still-wet hair, the journalist with the heels, who called almost every night from that west end cul-de-sac, a Montreal street so small, uninitiated drivers would argue with the dispatcher that it didn't exist. I was headed downtown, usually meeting Antoine at some dinner or opening. The Atlas car would always honk from precisely in front of the house, a standout facade among the row houses of avenue Bourgeois, white painted brick with black shutters, scarlet geraniums in boxes at every window in summer, miniature conifers in winter—a bit of an Edwardian dandy, just a *noticeable* house.

I'd come out with headphones already on, quickly voice the destination, and hope for the best. When it was good it was great, the cab swinging east over Mount Royal, the chandelier sky above and the velvet city appliquéd with skyscrapers below. Sometimes the city and the music and the silver disco moon would collide in a crescendo so exhilarating it felt like I was living in one of Antoine's classier commercials, and this is when—usually chemin de la Côte-des-Neiges—if it was going to happen, it happened: "Goddamned potholes! Goddamned city!" I'd say nothing, and hope the driver, in his front-seat world of aggravation, would work it out on his own. Sometimes my silence backfired and he'd put on his own music, so loudly it would shrill through my headphones, acid flung on my private film reel. It was always Arabic music. I assumed all the Atlas drivers were Lebanese. I assumed all Montreal Arabs were Lebanese.

THEY HADN'T HEARD from me in a year. Then I returned to them last winter. Always 10 a.m., always Mondays and

Thursdays, in a worn green canvas coat with a corduroy collar and a sensible hood, a knee-skimming jacket that was a country-weekend thing when I was well and now made me feel like a school-bus kid who had to dress with easy snaps. I used a tripod cane and carried with me a Paddington Bear cushion, an item that had been forgotten at our house by some friend's child and presently provided both a nice size and density for my automotive needs. I'd lie face down along the back seat, my nose in Paddington's taut belly. "I have had a severe neurological injury," I'd say—at this muffled juncture it was always *neurological*, the scariest word I could pull out of my hat—"please be very careful on the potholes."

For even the most relaxed drivers, the city became like a minefield. The ones with shit shocks tried it only once. Then the same driver started coming every time. I checked the laminated photo ID displayed in the felted space between the car's side windows. Mohammed Zandi. "What injury?" asked Mohammed, and I said, "Something like whiplash," a lie much easier than explaining that the skin of my spinal cord had decided to imitate Swiss cheese, that the operations had only made the holes bigger, that I was leaking spinal fluid until I had none, no cushion around my brain, soft brain knocking against hard skull, no buffer, and every car ride felt like a prelude to an aneurysm.

Mohammed drove me to a Chinese acupuncturist who tried to save drops of neurological water with tiny silver needles. Mohammed had a big white Mercedes with sporty tan leather seats. He also had a system. He would drive down Bourgeoys on the left side of the street, deftly avoiding what he termed the "roller ride" of the right, then he'd get onto avenue des Frères, hazards flashing, ten kilometres an hour, impervious to the symphony of anti-Mohammedan beeping that had descended on the street. "Who care!" he'd cry, waving and nodding with glee at the honkers. The street took us to avenue Girodet, a street freshly repaved by the city, and one we could take the whole way down, smooth as a magic carpet ride, a stretch like heaven.

After a couple of weeks, Mohammed wanted to know how I got home. "I can wait," he said, pointing to the acupuncturist's building. "Even wait hour. No problem."

But the rides back were my mother's job. Twice weekly, I'd endure the torture of a 1990 Hyundai Sonata, about as cushy as a medieval bear trap, containing a mum so nervous transporting me she'd expostulate Hebrew curses every time we encountered a crack in the pavement. "Sorry, sorry, *mamaleh*, there is nothing I can do!" she'd wail, speeding up instead of slowing down. Even the black marble of Girodet was jagged in my mum's tin jalopy, with its hard plastic interior and its filigree of flaking rust and its Tel Aviv bumper stickers and atmosphere of guilt so heavy I felt it on my eyelids.

After my last round of surgery, my mother retired. She had been the sort of travel agent who could get a passenger from Aéroport Dorval to Ben Gurion International via Warsaw via Frankfurt via Charles de Gaulle cheaper than any Internet outfit. She retired to take care of me. I had told her not to. At his advertising agency, Antoine was shooting another series of beer commercials, and those paid generously, and I still had some money to tide me over from when I was a staff writer. The weekly housekeeper, Mathilde, had agreed to come in every day—she gave me lunch, she changed the bandages, and she cooked dinner when Antoine came home. It was all figured out. I had decided I would have no nurse. I would especially have no mother—who was an expert in highly vocalized sympathy pains—as nurse. Not a mirror I needed, thanks.

I told Mohammed lifts back would be excellent. When I let my mother know about the arrangement, she said: "Ooooo-kehhh," in that singsong way that meant she was going to cry when she hung up and then call her sister in Haifa and grouse with outrage over how she'd retired for me, and I was so cold, and she thought we'd lie in bed and watch TV together, and—*ai!*—now she had such a migraine because I just didn't understand what it was like to have a daughter so sick; how much pain it gave her. If I knew, I'd be nicer.

MOHAMMED LOVED THE facade of the Bourgeoys house. He often commented on it when he dropped me off— the pristine white brick, the little conifers in window boxes. "But of everything, I like curtains the best," he said. "Good for taxi driver to look at when waiting." I was glad he noticed them, our living room blinds.

There were three leaded windows, and for a while we'd left them undressed. The living room was the site of much raucous interior decoration by Antoine and me, and we liked showing it off, even to pedestrians. It all started when Antoine found a stash of art gallery posters that his mother had collected when she was a teenager—Matisse, Picabia, Calder, a treasure trove— and we framed them all in shiny red lacquer. After that came an eighteenth-century sofa so large and so covered in cherry-pink velvet the dealer called it a "settee fit for a harem." We had bookshelves built all the way up a wall, and there was a shining brass Victorian fireman's ladder for reaching the top shelves. The room felt like a funhouse for heavy readers, and its winking refs continued into the powder room next to it, covered in a wallpaper that was like a collage of tabloid headlines from 1960s British sex scandals: *Would-be PM Takes the Mickey!*

I'd found that wall covering in a minuscule antiques shop on rue Notre-Dame. The store was owned by a frail woman who had the most transparent skin I'd ever seen and a real eye for vintage papers and fabrics. Antoine hated the paper at first, but after one prolonged use of the powder room he came round. "There are some situations," I told him, "in which it's good to have a little something to look at."

"We are going to have some fucked-up children with wallpaper like that!" he yowled in his weirdo English, pushing me up against the pink sofa, undoing my jeans from behind, mouth on my neck. It was going to be Beatrice for a girl, Maxim for a boy, and after we moved into Bourgeoys, they had a way of plopping into our conversations — out of nowhere, there'd be a baby sitting in the middle of a sentence.

The fabric for the living room windows came from the same shop. The owner remembered me. "You bought the sexy English wallpaper," she said, tapping the side of her head with a skeletal finger. "I remember. So today, it's for a baby's room?" "Not yet," I said, smiling, thinking about the dizzy spells I'd been having; the headaches and need for afternoon naps. It was possible. "Let's choose something fun anyway," I told the lady. "*Quelque chose un peu rigolo.*"

She had me heave it out from under a man's weight in other rolls. "A novelty textile from the turn of the century," she said, the cuffs of her cardigan quivering as she unrolled the dusty bolt on the cutting table. "This fabric will improve your view of the city." It was an irresistible pun—a material printed with a map of Montreal. "'The City of Montreal Corporation, 1890,'" she read off the fabric's corner. "Just *look* how so many streets didn't exist yet." The woman suggested I have Roman blinds made, the kind that fold up when you pull a string, instead of drapes. "When the blinds are down," she said, "you will see the pattern of the map perfectly."

AFTER COMING OUT of the hospital from the last round of procedures, I wondered if my wallpaper comment didn't comprise some sort of premonition. *There are some situations in which it's good to have a little something to look at.* The medics wheeled me from the medical tower, upright lab coats pushing some soft matter cocooned in blankets and morphine. On the yellow, day-lit street I saw amazing pedestrians flitting about, balancing takeout coffee and cellphones, talents they didn't even know were talents. On the sidewalk, the medical people were reminding my family that at home I should be furnished with an adjustable bed, "to facilitate mealtimes." The electric bed should be set up on a ground floor. Near a window is nice. "She can try walking to do toilet," said a nurse. "But mainly she'll need to be flat, for brain comfort. Her fluid will be highest in the morning, lowest at night."

My Bed-o-Matik arrived from a shop called Nuits Magiques. Antoine laughed heartily at the ugly, remote-controlled granny bed. "Next we will get one of those bathtubs with a door," he chuckled. This ribbing was Antoine's way. "You know, like they advertise on your Larry King." Ho, ho, suddenly geriatric American shows that weren't even on television anymore were "mine." Antoine wasn't prepared for this, me as mute blanket slug, nights radioactive with pain, him with his lifestyle flashing before his eyes.

Although he did know where to put the bed. He undid the stop latches of the bronze wheels that footed the cherry sofa and pushed the couch to the far end of the living room. The delivery men were instructed to position the Bed-o-Matik along the front wall, with its three windows and blinds of Montreal looking out onto Bourgeoys. The long, boxed radiator beneath the windows became my warm bedside table. Antoine had stacked it with fine, fresh notebooks of slippery European paper, and a second-hand *War and Peace*, an orange paperback brick sitting there like an old joke — *good time to read* War and Peace — and a new taunt — *just try to lift it*. "Nice books," explained Antoine, "so your brain won't rot."

I couldn't parse a printed page. I kept the blinds closed and looked at those instead. I could see the sun's position through them. When it filtered through the Molson estate, warming the belly of my brace, Mathilde brought my lunch. When it illuminated the corner of avenue des Pins and rue St-Denis, I had a hot drink and a change of bandages. When it lit past Papineau, entering the deep east end of the city—the blue ribbon of the St. Lawrence to the south—it meant the roaring waves of excruciation, the indescribable sensation of a brain sinking waterlessly, were closing in. Flatness won't help you now, take the pills, *ma petite*, don't be a martyr.

I loved my window map. I made friends with its antique lines the same way a kid blinking under cartoon sheets adopts the baby stalactites in a stucco ceiling or the knotted faces in wood panelling. I once even asked Antoine to turn the Bed-o-Matik around so that I could get a better view of the third window, with the fabric showing the fat blue vein of the St. Lawrence. "So you are finally finished with Bellefontaine?" he asked.

Bellefontaine was right in front of my eyes when I lay with my chin on my shoulder, head tilted towards the first window. In the map-making year 1890, this immense acreage belonged to the Sulpicians. Only one road—avenue des Frères—fed into the Catholic green from the forests and farms to the west. I was fascinated by des Frères's singularity in destination. There were no streets flanging out from it—no Girodet, no Bourgeoys. I imagined slow, pious feet walking in orderly single file, farm boys and sturdy sons of lumberjacks following the path. Every night, when Antoine came with the pills, when the pain was already curling everything in, I wanted to know, "Antoine, when will I be able to go to Bellefontaine?"

Antoine was surprised by the persistence of the question. Bellefontaine was entirely unromantic as dream location—just up the block from our house, and the site of a venerable bit of civic squabbling. The Sulpician land had long become home to a convent of Grey Nuns, and the nunnery had long been dwindling. Bellefontaine was so vast as to encompass its own *forest,* certainly too much for the nine remaining sisters to keep up, yet they guarded their territory with fearsome determination. The nuns would not sell a cubit to the city or to the needy school board, and they would not allow the borough access. There was a tall, point-topped iron fence that protected Bellefontaine, miles of erect iron arrows dotted with hand-lettered Proprieté Privé signs. The fence swept all the way down to the top of Bourgeoys, where there was a hole, two bars missing, easy trespass.

Before I became ill, I liked to take my mother's energetic spaniel there when the weather was warming or some article I was working on was not coming together. He would turn arabesques in the high grasses and I'd trace out where 150 years ago there were hedged gardens. He'd sniff the forest's border while I sat under a cedar and looked at the stone mother house, the old seminary, with its grand western hallway of Palladian windows, a passage that must have been lonely for the echo of steps. Sometimes I'd see a single nun. I'd smile and wave warmly. No trespassing sinner would wave so nicely and freely. *Please share your huge empty land with me.* The nun would usually smile back—a small, nodding smile through a six-foot window. *You, okay, but don't start telling the whole blessed borough.* So we had an agreement.

Antoine, when will I be able to go? First he said, "Soon." Then he said, "In a year." Then he said, "One day." As fall deepened into winter, I decided it was best to start keeping the blinds open.

MOHAMMED UNDERSTOOD MY need for strict regularity. No matter how deeply snowed the streets, he was never late. When a new and unavoidable pothole emerged on des Frères, he'd warn me in advance. And when he dropped me off at home, he'd wait in the car until I was in the vestibule and waving through the pane of the front door. He'd signal back, and only then would he drive off, making a nimble U-turn out of the cul-de-sac.

One day in late January, I noticed he didn't make the turn but just kept on going straight, something, I then realized, I'd seen before. What was Mohammed doing at the northern edge of Bourgeoys? I puzzled lazily over this small mystery. There wasn't much between the ending of the row houses and the fences of the nunnery. On the east side there was a quaint apartment building with a tiny, glass-fronted grocery store. A Middle Eastern family owned the nameless shop. Antoine, who is not exactly the king of political sensitivity, called the shop "Chez l'arabe." He thought this very Euro. "Everyone in Paris says they are going 'chez l'arabe,' even if their local store isn't owned by an Arab," he once informed my mother. "Well, the owners here are definitely not Jews," answered my mother, who added that no Jew would ever be so business-stupid as to open a shop at the closed side of a dead-end street. "After forty years in Quebec," said Antoine, hand cupping wise-guy mouth, "your mother still has sand in her shoes." My mother just nodded.

Across the street from Chez l'arabe was a park. I could see the park from my windows, a square with a few benches, almost a continuation of Bellefontaine outside its gates. I didn't see Mohammed loitering around there, and he didn't return to his car with groceries, either. It was a good half-hour before he drove out of Bourgeoys. I deduced that he must have been visiting someone in the apartment building. A sick relative, perhaps. He made her sugary mint tea and served it in a glass sashed with a folded paper napkin.

Mohammed thought it hilarious that I had given it any thought. Chez l'arabe had that winter introduced a hot-lunch bar. "Best lunch in the city," he said. "Wife makes. Favourite food of all Atlas taxi drivers." The shopkeepers brought out a few folding chairs every day at noon. "Homeland cooking," continued Mohammed. "Lamb stew, chicken with celery, saffron rice..." The owner's wife would sometimes save the crispy bark from the bottom of the rice pot for Mohammed. "Like a rice cookie!" he said, and I replied, getting into the spirit of the lunch excitement, that it sounded delicious, and so unlike the Lebanese food from most takeout places, the pitas filled with shaved, greasy chicken.

We were at a red light, the merest blush through layers of window steam and frost and white shards blowing from a low, gurning sky. The weather was so treacherous that Mathilde had fished an old purple ski pole out of the basement for me to use instead of the tripod cane. The leather crackled as Mohammed twisted his shoulder around to see me better. "It's not Lebanese food," he said, recognizing that I had his own nationality on the same plate. He was eyeing me in his back seat: a little girl and her bear cushion and silly pole. "It's

Persian food. Persian people. Like Atlas taxi drivers—all come to Canada in 1980s. Big immigration."

Just the walk from Mohammed's car into the clinic had me covered in white. "You very snow," said the Chinese acupuncturist as she helped me undress. She put the needles in, angled a heat lamp at my belly, and left the room. The room became arid. *Persians, Persians,* I thought, swallowing dryly. *Who were the Persians?* Enemies of the Jews in the Purim story. The seat of culture of the ancient Middle East. Invaded by Arabians. When? Dunno. Where? Not Iraq—we would have heard "Persian" on TV more often. Not Saudi Arabia, not Syria. I remember a neighbour with a baby stroller, the day we bought the house. *The corner store is very good, family run*—the stroller lady said it was a store owned by an older couple—*they have these fantastic giant cashews*—their daughter was a well-known journalist—*they also have these huge flatbreads, bread the size of a tabletop!*—she was twenty-five when she was imprisoned—*they said she was a heretic or a national threat or something*—she died on a hunger strike in jail—*a horror! Can you imagine being the mother?* Iran. God, when had I become so spacey? Of course it was Iran.

My rides with Mohammed ended abruptly. The acupuncturist said she wanted me to take a break from the needles. With the outings gone, my weekdays dribbled into each other, just time sludge. I recognized the weekends because I despised them. Mathilde was off, and Antoine was not ideal. He'd sequester himself in the TV room upstairs during the daytime and leave for parties at night— *"Petite,* where are my cufflinks?" "Do you think this scarf is too feminine?" —leaving me with extra painkillers. One Sunday he woke up at three-thirty in the afternoon, the sun already touching roofs. I had spent the day looking out the window, eating cookies from a box left on the radiator. "You spend all day looking out the window," he said, emerging in an open housecoat. He announced this as if my other option, the one I wasn't choosing, was going out flamenco dancing in a red dress. "Fuck, I think I'm hungover," he said, holding his forehead. He was wearing no underwear. I had forgotten what he looked like naked, so fuzzy. On languorous Sunday mornings in bed, I used to call him *mon gros nounours,* my big bear. "Fuck, I need coffee. Do you know if Mathilde remembered to get the organic milk?"

Mathilde had been forgetting all sorts of things. Her mother in Quebec City was in hospital. Then her mother in Quebec City was in need of home care. Soon enough, Mathilde went to Quebec City. Antoine left it to me to find her replacement. He was very concerned for our dinners. Antoine was a man who needed a proper plated supper, with an appetizer or a dessert and the right kind of wine. He said it wasn't too much to ask. But it was. I couldn't find new help, never mind the sort who could make choucroute the way Antoine liked and who knew which Brouilly was the good one.

Antoine was ordering us takeout and complaining every night that it was terrible. He'd put a box of glutinous beef in black bean sauce on my tray and then pretend he didn't hear when I called after finishing. "I'm watching a show for work," he'd say, eventually clomping in with eyes rolling, a fourteen-year-old forced to take out the garbage. He had become fanatical about watching animal documentaries in HD. He was developing an over-arty Darwinian theme for the beer commercials. "Tigers ruling the jungle, the bloody survival of the fittest!" he explained, scratching the air. "*Raaarrr!*" Antoine did not save the leftovers from the takeout food. Something about day-old Chinese in the house offended his sensibilities.

I SAT UP at eleven-thirty in the morning and counted. Eight row houses. Someone in the store will see my cane and will open the jingly-belled door. I will have ten dollars ready in my hand.

On your marks, get set . . . I couldn't get my socks on. *Fuck the socks.* I couldn't locate a bra. *Fuck the bra.* I had about twelve minutes until my brain hit my occipital bone; I didn't need supported breasts. Sweatshirt over brace, front zip, good. Hooded school-bus coat, snap, snap, done. Lowest hat on the coat tree, pompom, fine. Sweatpants riding up unshaven calves, lovely, lovely. *And ladies and gentlemen, she's off.* Left, right, keep going, one door, two doors, three — *slow and steady wins the race* — breathe, in, out, you are fine, fine — *she seems to be trying to speed up, ladies and gentlemen....*

Short-term memory loss is not uncommon among people with no brain suspension. I'd like to think that, sensorially deprived for so long, I walked into the shop and was lusciously overcome — swept away on a whirling mandala made of mastic candy and multicoloured veils. But I can't remember. I don't know how I chose from the hot bar or whether I left my ten-dollar bill crumpled on the penny saucer. I remember taxi drivers. I think I cut the line to give my order.

I woke flat-backed on the Bed-o-Matik, toes purpling in sopping sneakers. A sectioned foam takeout box, the kind with the lid that pops up too easily, was balanced on my belly, rising and falling with my breath. I curled my neck to see. There was lamb stew with saffron rice and a galette of the prized pot crust scraped off the bottom. Plastic cutlery was rolled up in a flimsy paper napkin and taped to the top of the box. When I finished eating, I sealed the box with the bit of tape, lifted my head an inch to aim, and tossed in the direction of the trash. Basket. Woo. I laid my head down again, thinking that it was the nicest food I'd had in a while, and that there was no way I could try that demented trip again.

The next day, I was just out of the living room, on a mission to extract baked beans from a can, when the doorbell rang. I recognized the foam box before I recognized the woman. She kept her eyes down. I was wearing an *Israel, Just Do It!* T-shirt, a fun sporty bootleg purchased in Tel Aviv's Carmel Market in 1990. In the fresh air, I smelled dog droppings, a smell of promise in this neighbourhood, the scent of thaw. "I can bring you lunch," she said. "Every day at noon, if you like. You may alert me to any food preferences." She looked up to see my reaction; for all she knew, I was a mute, in addition to being housebound and a supporter of human rights offences. *Just Do It!*

"Of course, I will pay you," I said.

"Yes, yes, certainly. At the end of the week is fine," she replied neatly, turning to leave. Under a forest-green Loden-style coat, she wore a neat beige skirt suit, the sort of outfit the nuns wore on days off, except she had no head covering over her short hair. "Thank you," I called out, a peculiarly Jewish brand of shame turning me yellow. A woman comes to my door as Kindness incarnate and I'm fanning bills.

Samira's lunches became an outsized part of my week. Antoine, too busy moping or primping for nights out at the clubs, didn't ask about my lunches, and so I didn't tell him. I liked having a secret. I'd watch Samira walking her quick, poised walk, as if she was running away from something, elegantly, every day at noon. My blinds were always pulled up then, but their bottom folds still formed a narrow town above the blue sky outside. Samira swam the St. Lawrence, hurled through the CP train yards, and whizzed through the borough of Verdun to get to my house. Samira was maybe five years older than my mother. She had studied medicine in Tehran in the 1960s. She didn't buy "something like whiplash," but didn't require anything more.

After a few weeks, I offered Samira extra money. "For coming all this way every day."

"Don't be silly," she said, placing the folded bill back on my lunch tray with her long, calm fingers. "I am only a few doors down. The walk takes one minute." It was a Tuesday. She had brought me cherry juice along with my meat and rice. The juice came in a stiff, shiny sack that you pierced with a thin, specially angled straw. She swiftly punctured the pouch and gently placed the juice near that day's takeout box. "I love the cherry juice," I said, licking my lips like a child making cutesy on a TV commercial. "Okay," she said, and glided out, Verdun, CP train yards, then passing my mother charging across Bourgeoys in stretch pants, yoga mat under her arm. My mother's steps reverberated through the house like a stampede.

"Where did you get that lunch?" she asked.

"The store on the corner."

"You know they have some Israeli food there — *labneh* and *zatar*."

"It's Persian food."

"*Labneh* is Israeli food."

"No, it's Middle Eastern food. Israelis eat it because their country is in the Middle East."

"I grew up eating *labneh*."

"Yes, and if the Jewish state had set up shop in Sweden, you'd have grown up eating lingonberries."

"What does Antoine call that store? Chez l'arabe?"

"They're not Arabs, they're Persians. Persians are not Arabs."

"You know they were a very cultured people, the Persians. Anyway, all the same now. Are you finished eating?"

"Yes."

"Give me — I'll eat the rest," said my mother. "Yoga was so hard today. I almost feel a migraine coming on. Still, your muscles feel so good after yoga, like your *inner* muscles." My mother said she had class again on Thursday. "It's just a few blocks away from here. An Israeli woman gives them in her basement." A grain of rice flew out of her mouth and onto the wood floor. I stared at it. "I'll come after," she said. "I'll bring your lunch."

"It's okay, they bring it."

"Who? The Persians?"

"The Persians."

"Tell them not to bother on Thursday. I'll pick it up. Do I give them money, or do you give them in advance?"

WHEN I WAS seventeen, I brought a new boyfriend home. It was then possible to have ten new ones in a year, but Tim must have been special because I hadn't brought the others in to meet my mother. Tim said he was "half Iranian"; maybe if he had used the term "half Persian," my mother wouldn't have looked up from her milky Nescafé the next morning, eyes still slitted with sleep, and said, as if weather-reporting:

"*Mamaleh*, it's in their blood."

"Who?"

"People like Tim."

"What?"

"The hatred."

This was the woman retrieving today's saffron chicken. A woman who believed the Jews invented *labneh*. She'd be in the shop in her yoga pants, preening her nationality before all the Atlas drivers, in needless self-defence. *It's in their blood./What?/The hatred.* She'd go into the store thinking *Iran*. Iran wants to nuclear-ize Israel to bone dust. I was trying to telepath her the message *They left*. Their daughter died in a fundamentalist jail. They never wore *Just Do It!* head scarves in bomb camp. They are from the seat of culture in the Middle East.

I had to keep my mother out of there. I fiddled with my bed controls. I flicked the side of the radiator over and over as if launching a fleet of miniature anti-mum fighter ships. I kicked off a slipper in frustration, and it flew across the living room and skidded under the cherry-pink sofa. Perfect. I was having a tantrum about my lunch delivery, and now my foot was going to be cold. She made everything so complicated.

I ate in silence and my mother watched me. She brought this too-thick mango nectar instead of the cherry juice that came with the strong little straw. I told her I was too tired to talk. She soon left.

The next day, Samira didn't come. For an hour, I looked out the windows for the neat suit carrying the white box. I saw people passing, walking their coffees and cellphones under high-floating clouds, never looking up at the white wonders pushing together, pulling apart, making and erasing holes of blue sky, nature always working so hard. I picked up the portable. The 411 operator said there was no listing for a store on Bourgeoys. "Are you sure it exists?" she asked. I dialed my mother's number.

Mom, I have no lunch.

"I have barley soup and cheese bagels," she said. "I'll be there in ten minutes." After I finished eating, my mother took the tray away. I watched her attractive, heart-shaped bottom as she walked to the kitchen. If I get out of this, I thought, that's what mine will eventually look like.

"You know, she didn't know you had a mother," she said, clattering in the kitchen. "The woman at Chez l'arabe. She said she didn't know about me." I didn't answer. My mother brought me tea, a bag mingling with mint in a glass with a rolled paper napkin tied around its middle.

"Did you tell them at the store that you were Israeli?" I asked

"I told them I was also Middle Eastern," she said.

"And?"

"And they wanted to know from where, so of course I told them we are Israeli."

Samira didn't come again. My mother brought my lunches, things she made, kugels and *bourekas*. I saw the birds arrive in V's through holes in the doily clouds and alight in the park outside Bellefontaine. I saw people taking their coffees for a walk. I saw ladies with strollers. I saw Samira sitting on one of the park's benches, outlined by a low disc of orange sun. I saw Samira wave warmly; I saw my mother wave back; I saw two women who had made an agreement.

DAVINA

IT MAY HAVE BEEN an old memory, coming up, or maybe
a composite of a few, blended by time. Anne saw oak
floorboards, richly polished, and speckled with the dry
confetti of trailed-in autumn leaves. She smelled the
deep amber of roast nuts and good whiskey by way of
breath, and the vinegary blue of night air rising from
wool coats just in from the cold. She could have been
remembering any number of dinner parties she'd
given, or any number she'd witnessed as a child, when
she loved hiding in the felted mass of guests' hung
coats, listening to the trills and haws of the adults in
the other rooms. Anne may have even been recalling a
dinner party she'd never been to, but rather one she'd
imagined for one of her books, a hefty table's worth of
titles (including the bestsellers *The Art of Entertaining,*

The Art of Entertaining Two, and *The Seasoned Hostess,*
now in its sixth printing). Anne's reputation as an expert, a guru of a recklessly baroque sort of domesticity,
was never a discomfort to her. Anne did not have moments of thinking she got away with something or of
feeling a fraud. Even the snobbiest chefs and critics who
had been to Anne's tiny, sloping, storybook house for
dinner parties agreed: not an ersatz situation. Anne
entertained deeply. She was the sort of hostess that
couldn't be faked.

And so here Anne was, at home, percolating with
the feeling of making another dinner party, possibly
her hundredth, but her first since her divorce from
Dan. Anne looked out her front window, at the gravel
drive that led to her front door. Her house was once the
servant's cottage belonging to a bootlegger's mansion
(a gabled fantasy that had been torn down in the 1940s),
and although now surrounded by solid city houses,
the cottage still enjoyed the privilege of a deep setting,
fronted by a long, old-fashioned drive, and an excellent
collection of maples. The trees were old, and generous
in their canopy. They had gone flame red in the last
week. Squirrels were spiralling up and down the corrugated trunks, preparing their nests.

Anne was thinking dense, somewhat grand food,
very close seating, too much of three kinds of wine, a
centrepiece of wood and berries, and her whole cottage

orange- and burn-scented with candlelight. She was thinking of the organic-produce importer she had lately been introduced to, the one who'd left banking for fanciful gourds and chanterelles and whose name — incredibly — was Fabrizio.

Fabrizio said he was an osso bucco man. Now, *this* was her type of person. It was endlessly fascinating to Anne how her greatest folly of youth had been in marrying too young. How she had donated all of her twenties, the whole decade, to Dan, a man who had grey, flaccid cells where his joy genes should be. Anne thought of how the preparations for this dinner would be so much more pleasant without her ex-husband's eyes rolling behind her back. In the months before the divorce, Dan couldn't even stand being in the vicinity of one of his wife's dinner parties. He'd grumble about "fairy dust" and "circuses." He'd sneer, "Who really *lives* this way?," some kind of puritanical ire spilling over. "*We* live this way when we have dinner parties," Anne would answer, waterproof, as she set and reset seating, arranged and rearranged cushions and crystal, melted down beeswax tapers so that they didn't look too fresh, and counted frosted curls of orange peel, needing the right amount for each dessert cup. This was, after all, her business.

ANNE'S EXPERTISE HAD developed through what she now views as an apprenticeship, the sort of education which comes with a lifelong debt of gratitude. She was given a taste for entertaining before she even had an interest in boys, and she got it from her father's second wife, Davina. Davina did not teach Anne by way of osmosis as much as through a slow and steady, mutually agreed-upon transmission. Anne remembers her first encounters with her stepmother's dinner party tables, how they contained so many splendid things. As a child, she could look at one of those wondrous tables for as many hours as she'd seen kids admiring train sets or dollhouses in basement rec rooms. To Anne, every row of silverware and every flower arrangement her stepmother laid out seemed permeated with some little, important, imported world of its own. There were tiny golden apples to hold place cards. There were minuscule silver cellars for salt. Davina was English, from England, which Anne understood meant more than just being an English *speaker*.

"Davina, what's that?" This was Anne, eight, on her tiptoes, pointing across the set dining room table to a silver tray on the sideboard.

"That's a sugar sifter."

"Why?"

"Because it's nicer to sprinkle sugar on your berries than to spoon the sugar on."

Anne still remembers how her stepmother upturned the turret-shaped sifter to show. "See how beautiful something as plain as sugar can be?" said Davina. Sparkling crystals fell out of the turret's slit top and bounced onto the white centre of a gold-rimmed plate. The gold-rimmed plate receiving the sugar was a salad plate. It nested on a bigger gold-rimmed plate, called a dinner plate. These plates were Davina's. Before marrying Davina and moving into her house, Anne's daddy had plates that said Dishwasher Proof in a clover on their underside. When he was still a single man, on the nights he had Anne, he'd put a container of individual-serve macaroni and cheese on top of the Dishwasher Proof plate for supper. Anne knew her daddy was a neuro, which meant a brain doctor; and also meant someone with a huge brain. She saw that he would rarely put a plate under his own macaroni container. He'd just hold it close under his chin, and softly shovel the food in as his eyes peered at the brain scans spread out on the kitchen table. Before marrying Davina, Daddy always had brain scans on the kitchen table. Davina, who said dinner deserves a dining room and was such a good chef that she didn't even have a microwave, said that when Daddy was a bachelor, he'd had the saddest suppers she'd ever seen.

ANNE WANTED HER table packed closely for her autumn party. She decided to squeeze in ten guests, with four singles (including herself and Fabrizio) and three couples. Couples were always the guest list problem. Anne knew this as well as any other experienced host. There was always a truly better half in a marriage, and often the more buoyant or sparkling that half, the more silent or introverted the other. It was counter-intuitive, but Anne found that couples with a few years behind them were better than fresh ones. The fresh were always so easily offended in their pristine patch of as-yet-unbroken eggshells. Old marriages had more shards about them, little edges of spousal vengeance, provocation, rivalry, the sort of stuff that could add intrigue to a room.

Anne had recently received a note from a couple just wedded, he a wine writer and she a big player in fair trade coffee, who had both been married to other people when they met at Anne's table. "We owe it all to your magical dinner," they wrote, apparently, together. "Your generosity as a hostess is a wonder."

Generous hostess. It was fascinating to Anne how often this was said. She didn't fool herself about it. Although she'd never write this in one of her books, Anne didn't think that the true spirit of the most suc-cessful hostesses—and there was a breed—was one of giving. The giving was incidental. Anne only needed to look at herself. Did she rush to fill a guest's empty wineglass because she is so compassionate that she couldn't *stand* the idea of someone having a drop less? The hosting impulse didn't come from so lilywhite a place. It came from a place of desire; a craving for beauty and order and comfort. There was reassurance in the idea that one could live so well, if only for one night.

For this dinner, Anne would remove the chairs from her dining room. She'd bring in the oak benches that she had for just this sort of occasion, where guests would need to touch. The benches were floor-scraping and heavy, but looked great with the room's drippy low-hanging chandelier and its thick refectory table, which took up at least three-quarters of the room's space. Anne didn't mind having a dining room that was all light and table, even if it meant that nary a dinner went by without at least one guest bonking the front of their head against the chandelier or the back of it against a wall.

Anne recalls one dinner party about a year ago: a table for six; duck with pears; Dan—as had become his custom—sitting it out in his office downtown. One of the guests was a youngish architect known for mercilessly scooping out the insides of heritage buildings or buttressing grand old dames with sharp, glassy, incongruous extensions. "What do you call that style? Victoriana with a bad case of glass?" bellowed one of Anne's guests, a famously nasty pastry chef. Anne hooted. She couldn't help it. It was a good line. The architect was offended. Ignoring the pastry chef, he went straight for Anne, telling her that her house "would give *any* modern architect—and by modern I mean *living*—hives! All these miniature overstuffed rooms. Walls just begging to be ripped down."

Anne felt secure in her taste. She thought architects were nuts for looking down on nooks and walls and corners. She could think of nothing less enticing than the open-plan, glass-curtain architecture that passes unquestioned as today's finest kind, where a life's backstage is forced to the front, into a dry expanse of space and white, and nothing is contained. Anne felt a tiny draft of trepidation as she began ushering her guests out of the dining room. She didn't want the night to wind down. She thought of Dan, alone in his office with a blinking computer screen in a featureless glass building. She thought of how only Dan could truly prefer that kind of blankness—a drooping sandwich out of plastic for dinner—over the splendid evening Anne had made.

AS A CHILD, when Anne drew crayon pictures, she always drew a frame around them. Daddy had once asked her why and she said "so the picture has its own room." In Daddy and Davina's house every room had a door, and some rooms even had their own hallway. Anne liked this, the way everything had its own place. Anne's favourite room in the house was her own bedroom. It was on the third floor. Its walls and curtains were covered in pink vines and trellises and a border of minuscule buds. Two small white bookcases flanked her bed. Their shelves contained Davina's books from when Davina was a girl: cozy English-garden animals in jackets with brass buttons and all the drawings done in fine wispy lines. Anne was a little old for those books. Although once in a while, after being tucked in, she'd pretend she wasn't and would read to herself. Mostly, she was too hyper to read in bed. She'd sit up in her flannel nightie, all abuzz, eyeballs pitched to darkened ceiling, and repeat things, quickly, as if there was a clock ticking, and only so much time to capture the information.

Four-course place setting, left to right: Left side: small fork, big fork, small fork. Right side: small knife, different small knife, spoon, big knife, small knife. Goose fat makes the most golden roast potatoes. Raspberries are best unwashed. People in Canada will never understand the meaning of real cream. Daisies are poor flowers. When you are finished eating, put your knife and fork together on the plate, like husband and wife.

In the evenings, Davina would sit in the drawing room, which was the length of the floor below Anne's bedroom. The drawing room had its own staircase of loopy-loop brass curls and there was wood panelling that went zig and zag in a pattern called herringbone. There were lots of chairs and polished tables with feet that looked like paws or like claws. There were two sofas covered in something called damask, and lots of paintings grouped closely, hung one on top of the other. Davina liked to sit in the drawing room even on nights when she wasn't entertaining. She would read things on one of the sofas or she would write things at her secretary.

Davina's secretary was not a person like Daddy's secretary, who was a mean lady at the hospital with yellow-coated teeth. Davina's secretary was a shiny black desk with carved, pearly Chinese flowers going up its sides and lots of different-sized drawers and slotted sections and a tiny golden railing up top. Anne sometimes played that Davina's secretary was a little girl's house, with a selection of rooms and storeys, and the golden railing a balcony to keep the little girl's finger-doll friends from falling off.

"Davina…" This was Anne, in her nightie, down from her bedroom, not sleepy.

"Yes, dear? Do you know it's almost ten?" This was Davina, at her secretary. She was writing with a fountain pen on a piece of thick grey-blue paper. That meant a thank-you note.

"Did you ever have a dinner party with a frog in a bow tie?" asked Anne.

"No, dear, that's only in storybooks."

"I heard Daddy call some man a toad, after a dinner party. He said" — and here Anne drew her voice down, and flung out her arm, like a Victorian actor — "'I don't care who he is! He's a toad!' and you said, 'Well, I think he's a *fascinating* toad...'"

"I can see you are not tired," Davina said. Anne was now on the floor, hopping around like a frog. Anne knew she was being hyper. She was often hyper at night. She couldn't help it, she felt funny things. "Rib-bit!" said Anne. Davina was shaking her head, but she was not displeased. She was wearing wine-coloured shoes with high heels. Davina always wore shoes in the house, and also stockings that were so see-through you barely saw them at all. You had to know how to look. Anne knew that with the best things, it was often like that. "Come down to the kitchen," said Davina, putting away her correspondence. "I'll make you some banana milk."

Davina said *banoner* even though *banana* had three *a*'s. Anne boinged down the stairs behind her step-mother. "Banoner! Banoner!" She could never make it sound like Davina made it sound. "Banernerrrrrrr!"

"Shhh!" said Davina, widening her eyes at Anne. "Daddy won't like me having you awake." Daddy was in his office upstairs. Anne wasn't allowed to bother him there unless it was very *essential*, because he needed to be alone and quiet with his brain scans and his computer.

In the kitchen, Davina had a bookshelf full of books about cooking and entertaining. Anne took out her favourite and tucked into the kitchen banquette with it. The banquette was covered in a striped fabric called mattress ticking, because it was the fabric you found on beds a long time ago. The book was called *Dinner Parties in Style*, and Anne must have looked at it, sitting in the kitchen, studying the same black-and-white photographs, a thousand times. Her favourite stylish party-givers in the book were Mrs. Afra Gottlieb, who liked to mix modern art with antiques in her New York penthouse, and thought the most exciting meals were Middle Eastern; Mr. Benjamin Deacon, a handsome bachelor who did all hors d'oeuvre dinners under hundreds of paper lanterns strung up in his East Hampton beachfront; and Lady Antonia Anson, who once gave an indoor picnic, complete with huge striped blankets and chilled chicken drumsticks, on the floor of her Belgravia townhouse.

Davina, who said *Belgravier* even though it was spelled with two *a*'s, knew Lady Antonia Anson from university in England. They had dated the same man. Davina said that the man had been the youngest don ever at her university. Anne did not know what the word "don" meant and chose to imagine it as a sunrise, a dawn. Davina and Anne sometimes saw the man on television. He had a beard and lots of teeth and a bow tie and he was always talking excitedly about art in front of a very old building in Italy or Greece. Davina said that the man was brilliant in a way that lit you up and that you could never forget. If he was coming to your dinner party, she said, you'd save him the most important place at the table.

At the banquette, Anne was dividing her attention between looking at *Dinner Parties in Style* and at her stepmother. Davina stood at the counter, peeling a banana. Her sweater was form-fitting and plum coloured, reminding Anne of Davina's perfume, which smelled like deep purple, and Davina's favourite flowers, which looked like they grew somewhere darker than an open field. Davina puréed half a banana with the back of a fork, expertly. She then pressed the mash through the fork's tines by pressing down with a spoon, making the pulp even finer. Davina stirred the fruit to a froth in a specially chosen milk glass, wide and bevelled. "Here you are," she said. "Double yummy, so hold it with both hands."

"I like the glass," whispered Anne, who had grown

more tired and bed-ready but still felt how good the heavy glass felt in her fingers and how soft the banana tasted in the milk. Anne was on the page in the book with the photograph of Lady Antonia Anson. Lady Antonia Anson had hair like a lion's mane and crinkles at the sides of her eyes as if she laughed a lot in the sunshine.

"Davina," asked Anne, still looking at the photo. "If you married the man from your university, would I still know you?" Anne had the cold, empty feeling of putting words together that she couldn't imagine the meaning of. "I think it's too late for such silly questions," said Davina. That night she let Anne get under the covers with the book from the kitchen. In bed, Anne didn't snuggle it like a teddy but arranged it open on her chest, as if her heart could absorb its pages. "I like it like this," Anne said as her stepmother turned out the bed-side lamp. The book's spine peaked over Anne's small rib cage like the top of a little house. As long as it was there, Anne felt, there was nothing to be afraid of.

UNLESS SHE NEEDED to order some exotic fowl or uncommon cut, Anne tried to leave the planning of a dinner party's menu as long as she could. It was important to her what the week felt like, what the weather looked like. Sitting at the head of the refectory table in her dining room, she took a piece of notepaper out of its drawer. The dining room was painted the colour of dark wine: chandelier on, the deepest grape purple, chandelier dimmed, an enveloping black. The room had two sash windows, and from where Anne now sat, they were completely filled with flame-red maple leaves. Heartbreaker leaves, thought Anne, most beautiful when about to detach and fall. She'd save this seat for Fabrizio. At night, the red of the leaves would look a blackish burgundy, nearly matching the colour of her walls. The menu wrote itself:

Consommé royale with morel mushrooms
Veal chops with port glaze
Red new potatoes
Purple kale with crispy pancetta
Fennel salad
Orange confit ice cream
Dark chocolate nougat, coffee

A squirrel had hopped onto a window ledge outside Anne's dining room, gripping a large chunk of olive bread, clearly poached from Anne's trash bin. With autumn's deepening, the squirrels were working harder and harder to kit their nests. It annoyed Anne that trash bins were difficult to buy in proper metal anymore. Bins now came in thudding, dun-coloured plastic and were called "heavy duty" and the squirrels nibbled large holes into their tops as if into marzipan. Anne watched the squirrel and the olive bread. It was windy outside, and the animal's fluffy tail was parting to the pink skin. Well, let the squirrels have nice bread, she thought. Why not make it easier on them? Once, when she was a girl, she was outside strolling with her father, when right before their eyes, a squirrel fell to the sidewalk from a tree. The animal lay on her back, twitching. Anne has never forgotten the sound of the squirrel hitting the ground, a fleshy plop. "What happened?" she had asked her daddy, her upper lip trembling. "She was making her nest in the tree," Daddy said, steering his eight-year-old daughter away from the dying squirrel. "She just fell." Anne couldn't tell from this answer if it was a normal occurrence for squirrels: nest-making one minute and flat on the pavement, animal refuse, the next. "Maybe it was the wind," he said.

It had probably been blowing hard—*a howling gale*, Davina would say. Daddy loved the windiest days, weather most people would stay in for. Davina said that this was because Daddy was the type of man who liked to stand on mountaintops and get his hair blown around. Anne knew Davina didn't mean real mountains, or real hair (because Daddy had almost none). But Anne understood. She could feel a quality in her Daddy, something, like moving air; something that couldn't be held. When Daddy was working extra hard in his top-floor office, he'd listen to music that had the same feeling, only in sound. When he played it, it meant he was writing an article on his computer (an article so difficult, only other neuros could understand it), and Anne wasn't allowed to tiptoe up for any reason whatsoever, even a good-night kiss. Anne would hear the sparse music as if it was lancing its shardlike notes into her bedroom. It wasn't the glassiness of the sounds that frightened her. It was the spaces between them — too wide, too quiet. Anne liked the parping horns and fanciful strings at the Sunday children's concerts that she'd been to with Davina. She once had a macabre fantasy, like a scene from a scary movie, that if she did sneak up to Daddy's office when he had his music on, she might find him there with the skylight torn off the ceiling, typing furiously in a spiralling wind of scans and papers, a white light erasing all the normal details.

IN HER BOOK *The Art of Entertaining,* Anne wrote that the best thing a host can do for an event is to run around as little as possible right before it. Never shop the day of. Set the table the night before. A long and relaxing bath before the event is a must. "Remember," wrote the expert Anne, "stress is poison to the party. A harried host ruins the roast."

Anne still had a softened piece of grey-blue card, a list she'd found as a child, stuck between two sections of her stepmother's secretary.

> *Thu.*
> *Lessard & Fils delivery noon*
> *—Call in am for extra herbs*
> *Menu—see attached pg 1. most imp. meat in marinade by 4pm*
> *Evening: Check table setting/service*
>
> *Fri.*
> *Menu—see attached pg for staff*
> *Florist delivery 3pm*
> *Wine uncorked 4pm*
> *Bath 4:30pm sharp—REST UP!*

To Anne's own satisfaction, she still used Lessard & Fils, the same shop patronized by Davina, a store Anne had been taken to many times as a child. M. Lessard had gone, but Jean-Paul Lessard—his son; the *fils*—remained, his father's apprentice, a fount of bottomless know-how reconstituted. The shop remained a jewel-like emporium in the old food hall tradition, with runner beans and squash displayed as if mounding from an overflowing treasure chest, and cornucopias of kumquats and lychees, and herbs tied into bunches with cotton string, and glass cabinets of twinkling confections, and shelves of crusty bread and meat displayed as if ruby slabs (which went home in thick brown paper, never sweating under plastic). There was a cheese smell so old and pungent upon entry, it could qualify as both an experience and a triumph of context. The shop delivered in square baskets woven from a sturdy rattan as thick as tree branches. The baskets would seem an old-tymey gimmick aimed at lifestyle shoppers, but were in fact the very same baskets used for delivery in the senior Lessard days.

When Davina would enter Lessard & Fils, M. Lessard would always cry, *"Bonjour, Madame Davina!"* and Davina would respond, *"Enchantée comme toujours, M. Lessard,"* as if M. Lessard was the one to be honoured, exchanging such bounty for mere money. Anne would stand happily in the shop in her little blue coat and white tights while Davina discussed a list with M. Lessard. M. Lessard would be wearing a long striped smock, and had a walrus moustache, and looked like something out of one of the children's books in Anne's bedroom. *Here is the shopkeeper in his striped smock. The shopkeeper leaves a little piece of cheese for the mouse family snug in the wall. Here is the mommy mouse in her smart hat, and here is the baby mouse in her little blue coat.* Anne sometimes felt her heart beat hungrily in the store, her eyes filling with so many nice things, sweets and buns and cakes, and everything so tightly and prettily arranged.

"Davina?" This was Anne, leaving the shop with her stepmother, nibbling on a jelly covered in sparkling sugar granules.

"Swallow before speaking, dear."

Anne swallowed. "Davina, what's a materialist?"

"Did your father give you that word?"

"I don't know."

"It's quite a word!"

"Is it bad?"

"Some would say so."

"Are you one?"

"Well, I love beautiful material. Wood and flowers and lovely jellies from M. Lessard."

"Me too! Like this purple one!"

"— and that's different from just wanting a lot of things. Some people just want a lot of things, but they don't care about them. That's not a very nice way to be."

"So there is a good kind?"

Davina said: "I don't see why anything should be considered less meaningful just because it's concrete. We live in a concrete world, after all." Anne knew that Davina didn't usually speak this way, so urgent and yet complicated. A child can pick out words honed in a fight.

"Is Daddy a materialist?"

"Your father doesn't love too many things he can actually see."

"Can I be one?"

"Well. Only the good kind, dear." Davina squeezed Anne's hand, a nice warm squeeze, leather glove to woolly mitten. "That means that you will have to work very hard at it."

ANNE HAD A lot to discuss with Jean-Paul Lessard. She was not making a show-offy osso bucco for Fabrizio—that would be too much, too soon. But she was doing veal, so she needed the veal to be *spectacular* veal, a sign of the marrow to come. She wanted the chops cut abnormally thick—Jean-Paul Lessard, a traditionalist, would find it barbarous, but Anne was going for high drama. Also, she was thinking of altering the orange confit ice cream that she always ordered from the shop to include almonds. Orange confit ice cream was a year-round tradition at Anne's dinner parties. When Anne had her oldest friends or relatives over to dinner, they remembered it as having been one of Anne's father's second wife's signatures as well. Davina had invented the recipe one autumn day, when the maple leaves were flame red and Anne was by her side, in her little blue coat and white tights.

"*M. Lessard, avez-vous des oranges confits?*"

"*Oui, Madame Davina!*"

"Et votre fabuleuse crème glacée à la vanille?"

"Oui, Madame!"

Davina said she felt like creating something original that day. "A new invention!" she said. "Candied orange ice cream."

Anne spoke loudly, the way an outraged child does, a child that senses something is wrong, a fissure in the normal. "Davina, Daddy *hates* orange candies—he says orange candies taste like medicine!" Anne also knew her father liked plain ice cream, just white. Anne had been taught that it was useful to remember tastes like that. Some dislike curry, or cooked-fruit desserts, others don't eat meat, the hostess must be aware.

"Your daddy," said Davina, "will be too busy with his work to join my dinner party."

Not long after, Anne's daddy went to live on the top floor of a high-rise near the river. His condominium had glass walls on all sides and a view of the sky and on a clear day the mountains beyond the city. The sound of the wind up high was like ghosts skimming the glass. Sometimes the outside air would get in. It would flow like an invisible layer over the flat grey carpeting. Anne wore heavy socks even in the summer. Anne's bedroom was a white colour called "Icedrift" and had very flat, hard modern furniture, all attached and built in. There was a pool in the basement with a spooky echo and water that burned Anne's private parts.

Sometimes, on a school bus, returning from a field trip to the museum or the arboretum, Anne would catch a glimpse of Davina's house. She'd make her eyes alert and ready to look up the street when she knew it was coming. One day, Anne thought, I will get there. I will go, and I will have banana milk with Davina, and I'll sleep in my pink bed, and it will be a secret. But Anne was just eight, then nine, just ten, eleven, and subject to her parent's sense of propriety. And then Anne was a teenager, and it was easier not to care.

When Anne married Dan, the man whom she had married too young, a man too much like her father, a man she was now divorced from, Davina sat in the middle ground of the chapel. Davina: near minor cousins and neurologists with their wives, a vision in a sculpted suit and an Ascot-worthy hat bearing a cluster of tiny silken fruit. As Anne walked down the aisle, her eyes searched for and found her ex-stepmother's eyes. The two women exchanged knowing looks, their bond still there, their reading of the situation identical: *We both know how this event will end.*

"DAVINA." THIS WAS Anne, sitting near a stack of suitcases and brown boxes, *Dinner Parties in Style* on her eight-year-old lap, moving truck outside. "What will we be when you aren't my stepmother?"

"We will always be a pair, Anne. Because we are so alike."

WRAPPING A PLUM-COLOURED wool scarf around her neck, Anne imagined Fabrizio in her dining room, enjoying her food and wine. There was nothing better than a man who noticed, who knew what to notice. Anne pocketed her list for Lessard & Fils and saw, from the quality of sunlight, that it was a crisp day. She fished a pair of leather gloves out of a drawer in her front closet. It was good to put on gloves for the first time in months, the way the dyed skin stretched tight over the hand, the knuckles shiny. Grabbing her house keys, she found her heart beating excitedly as she opened her front door and a few red leaves came in. Anne breathed in the woodsiness of the autumn air. It was the best time of year for a dinner party.

APPALACHIAN SPRING

THERE WERE SEVEN FAILED surgeries and then there was one that was called a success. A neurosurgeon scooped flesh out of my left lateral dorsal muscle. He then pushed and sewed and stapled those corks into the places where my spinal cord had ripped, where the spinal fluid had been leaking, long depriving an increasingly sagging brain of its rightful waterbed. With these new dams in place, the surgeon said that for a few weeks I might even have a little too much spinal fluid, and that this would be a novel situation for my brain, which had become, as he'd put it, "used to living in the driest skull this side of the Mojave."

Within a few days, I was wheeled out of hospital. It was the end of winter in Montreal, the sky the colour of overcooked veal, and I was encased in a zipped, full

torso made of elastic and stamped BINDING COMPRES-
SION GIRDLE (POST OP) across its side. There was a gus-
set bearing appropriate slits for elimination. I stayed in
the guest bedroom of the house I shared with my husband, a terraced Edwardian on a cul-de-sac, which had,
in my absence, turned on me with its multiple staircases and tapering horizon of neighbours with large
windows. In the daytime, my father came over and
sat in the den across from my bedroom, and nervously
tapped on his laptop with his ears pricked. My husband
was on night watch. In the evenings, the changing of
the guard was ceremonialized with Bloody Caesars. I'd
hear my husband and my dad talking in hushed tones
about me over their drinks in the study downstairs. I
heard my father weeping once. At first I thought it was
because only a few months had passed since he'd lost
his mother, my grandmother, but then I heard him saying, "It's just, you know, when it's *your child . . .*"

The surgeon said that, aside from a few fringed
nerves and the possible intracranial fullness, I was to be
good as new inside a few weeks. The baroque crotch-
less unit was soon replaced with a simpler corset, and I
found that I no longer had the problems that had belea-
guered me when I was leaking spinal fluid: the daily
shutdown as my sagging, unsuspended cerebellum hit
the hard saucer of my occipital bone. I was a woman
alive. So there was frustration, in the family, that I still

wasn't bouncing back to normality as I should have. I would pre-empt efforts to foist guests on me by putting yellow Do Not Disturb notes on the bedroom door. When I did emerge from my room, clinging to the walls instead of using the metal cane assigned to me in hospital, I was observed so carefully that I came out increasingly rarely, and usually only to go to the bathroom.

The decision to leave came in mid-May. I know this from my credit card files. I had been in the bathroom, taking a bit longer than usual with a pee. "Everything under control?" asked my father through the door. I could hear him breathing in the hallway. Rigid on the toilet, I recalled a girl I had known in my late teens. One night she got so fucked up in a nightclub that she lifted up her skirt, pulled down her underwear, crouched in her high heels, and began peeing on the dance floor. When I first heard this story, I thought that I had never heard anything more humiliating. I touched the hard wall in the bathroom. *I am in my house.* I leaned over and locked the bathroom door. *And when I leave this room, I will have a plan of escape.*

Earlier that week, I had read what I can now assure you, because I have since looked it up, was an unremarkable 600-worder in the newspaper travel section, a story about Ojai, California. In the article, Ojai is described as a place with a marvellous climate, a free-spirited classical music festival, and an impressive pedigree among bohemian cognoscenti and various classes of seekers. The illustration is a photograph of the spiritual leader Jiddu Krishnamurti, who, in the 1930s, shucked off his fusty East Coast patrons to become a freelance guru in Ojai. In the picture, Krishnamurti is wearing a suit and is sitting on a chair with one leg draped over the other. A few disciples are lounging on cushions at his feet, beatific in their peasant shirts and moccasins. The excellent Californian mountains make up the background. *The Ojai Valley*, reads the photo caption, *a Shangri-La of West Coast Enlightenment.*

Ojai instantly captured a singular spot in my mind's geography. It wasn't only that my brick house in Montreal instantly seemed the opposite of exotic in comparison, but also that Ojai was so different from the other parts of California I'd known. My father's mother used to winter in Palm Springs. She had a stand-alone unit at the antisocial end of a faux pueblo condo complex where widows liked taking the sun together, playing pinochle by the pool. If there was an old lady who wintered in Ojai, I thought, she'd be of a different ilk. She'd be the type to wear a long grey braid and grow mums. You'd see her serenely comparing herbal tea boxes at the health food store. She'd have many friends and former lovers, she'd be an etcher, a potter, a weaver, or an expert in Japanese calligraphy, a woman with a well-worn meditation cushion and an intriguing education, somebody *fascinating*.

I TOOK A metered cab the whole eighty miles from LAX to Ojai, fading in and out from the pharmacopoeia I'd ingested for the cause of flying across the continent. I was using medical-marijuana spray as if it were nothing more than a camphor inhaler. The blood vessels in my skull had begun feeling hotly blimped out, as if broiling calluses onto the edges of my brain. I could not feel the backs of my calves, and soon not my heels, and my left arm was like a phantom limb made flesh. The cab driver had a tattoo on his neck that looked like the sort of scripty thing you'd get in prison. He said he lived in Meiners Oaks, a less ritzy part of Ventura County. When he brought my bag into the house I'd rented, he peered into the hallway and said, "Sweet place." I answered, with what I felt to be superb casualness, "Yes, we've always loved it here." What royal "we" I had in mind I have no idea, but I didn't want this prison-tattoo man getting the impression that I was to be a solitary presence in this little house in Ojai.

I had rented the house back in Montreal at Bloody Caesar hour, in a five-minute crapshoot of heroic financial recklessness and Internet faith. The rental ad had said, "Original 1930s California Bungalow," and the pictures had been vague—a view through a window, a made bed. I was prepared for some seediness. But as the stone path leading to the house came into view, I was reminded of a feeling I'd had a few times, in what seemed a different life, when I'd been sent somewhere on a magazine assignment and the hotel responded with a room more lavish than anything ever expected. I remembered one overly modish hotel suite in Los Angeles. Entirely orange, with its own roof deck, it had a six-foot, slate-grey, plasticized foam sculpture of a foot in the middle of the bathroom. It was truly a design move for assholes—*Darling, my bathroom is so insanely big it can fit a six-foot foot in it.* On the hotel phone, I called the photographer who had flown in with me. "You have to come up and see this place," I said. I needed him as witness. I'd return to Montreal and no one would believe me.

This Ojai house was impressive in a better way. A square single-storey villa of pristine wood shingle with a red-painted door hung with a ceramic knocker, it was bordered the whole way around by a stone verandah. The verandah led to an open, brushy field on one side, and on the opposite side to a garden whose main feature was a massive storybook tree with an octagonal bench circling its base and wind chimes hanging off a low branch. Out back was an orange grove hemmed by a white picket fence. The name of the hilltop street was

Mountainview. The Topa Topa Mountains shone pink in the close distance.

The inside of the house had been redone entirely. The bathroom was in an almost veinless marble and the kitchen was a sanitized Provençal with plates in slots over a giant country sink. There was a fridge the size of a walk-in closet and floors in buffed wide hardwood. There were French doors leading from the dining room to the garden with the ancient tree.

How pristine it all was. So pristine that, after a few days, I was harbouring a persistent curiosity about the house's usual resident, an Ojai real estate agent named Beth Dooney. I put her in her late forties. She had mentioned more than once in our brief email correspondence that she was "journeying" to Italy for the eight weeks I was occupying her house. She'd intimated that the trip was awfully well deserved, perhaps coming in the wake of personal crisis, by giving her emails headings such as "gelato for breakfast here i come." The house's interior certainly pointed to some kind of transition. It was full but still oddly blank as a place to call home, lined with the kind of mid-range, blackish-brown wood furniture that comes in collections called New Horizons or West Contemporary. Everything looked box-fresh. The plates were chipless white, the sheets and towels flawless white. There was no old, ugly crystal vase from a dead aunt or bowl of pennies silted with lint and paper clips. The closest thing to a standard junk drawer was one in the kitchen that slid open easily to display corks in a zippered plastic bag, a pair of binoculars in a black nylon case, and garden scissors in a spotless suede holster. There were no photos. On a sideboard I saw two New Horizons–ish picture frames, but they contained identical photos of sunsets.

I guessed that my lessor was doing Italia alone. I began forming a deeper backstory: the victim of a painfully dissolving marriage, her therapist told her to get out fast. Her energy healer concurred. Leave it all! So she walked out of her emotionally abusive husband's life and straight into Pottery Barn.

The bookshelves also looked like they had been stocked on a single trip to the mall. There were mainly self-help books: *The Power of Now*; *Your Life Now*; *The Present Is a Gift*. A single row of CDs consisted almost entirely of the kind of music formerly known as "whale," now rebranded as "spa." The only tangent was a Boston Pops CD called *American Visions*. I looked at the track listing on the back. The disc contained what I remembered as my grandmother's favourite piece of orchestral music, Aaron Copland's paean to big, open-air America, *Appalachian Spring*. My grandmother first discovered it, I'm sure, because it's what the Plattsburgh TV station that she watched in Montreal used to play after the national anthem when they stopped broadcasting at 3 a.m. When I was a kid, the music thrilled me as well because it contained a passage I recognized from a dog food commercial; terriers pulling Chihuahuas in chuckwagons.

I liked to put the Copland track on and stand on the verandah, looking out. I knew the Appalachians were not Californian mountains; still, the Topa Topas felt like a painted set for this exact piece of music. It did gnaw a little that I couldn't remember where the Appalachians actually *were*. Virginia? Colorado? I hadn't brought my computer with me and couldn't very well ask anybody. There were acres buffering me from my neighbours, and you couldn't see most of their houses from the road. Some properties had electric gates. There were never any strolling locals, just the occasional SUV whizzing by.

Before long, I was relieved by this. I had arranged for a human event every few days — a delivery guy who arrived with bags of food from a shop in town that I'd found in the Yellow Pages — and I was even uneasy with him in the house. In setting up my account with the store on the telephone, I'd said I was caring for an old woman, a completely spontaneous and unnecessary lie. When the delivery guy arrived, I had to keep the bedroom door portentously closed.

"She's bedridden," I explained, with the appropriate look of caregiving compassion on my face.

The delivery guy told me his wife also took work looking after the infirm, and I said, "Oh, I don't do this for money." Seeing the way my hand trembled when giving over bills, and then spotting the corset under my polo shirt, he said, "Well, you must be a very kind woman, helping someone when—" and he pointed his chin at my midriff. "Must get tough," he said, "you guys up here by yourselves."

My being alone seemed to be of universal concern to every person I had any contact with. When I spoke to anyone back home, they had words about it, so many words that I soon remedied the situation by unplugging the phone and putting it in a cupboard, its wire neatly coiled and secured with a twist-tie. The last person I'd spoken to had been one of my magazine editors. I had tried to sound like an adventurous woman on a fabbo mountaintop retreat. "Are those *wind chimes?*" he'd asked, having none of it. I imagined him looking out of his plate-glass window, onto the teeming street below, and thinking another one of his writers had lost the plot, or their mind, before managing to make anything big of themselves.

I was in no condition for any exploratory walkabouts in Ojai. I couldn't really bring myself to step beyond that verandah. The plugs and staples sealing my spinal cord had definitely screwed up some nerves. Since arriving, I felt like I was wearing rocking Dutch clogs. My left arm was a bloodless husk and my right hand, a rusty lobster claw. With my spinal cord continuously overfilled, the pressure in my head was a new world of weird. Any exertion that made my heart beat quickly made one of those magician's wiener balloons blow up around my brain, squeezing stars into my eyes, bells into my ears, and once or twice knocking me out from sheer excruciation.

The neurosurgeon had said I needed to be sensitive to what my body was telling me post-operation. One wrong move and I could pop his corks out, making bigger holes, worse leaks, geysers. But things were in such an uproar that I often couldn't tell pain from tingling and tingling from numbness. I would close my eyes, touch body parts, and ask: *Can I feel this? What is this?*

Every so often a vision of my grandmother, a woman in nightclothes padding slowly through a condo, shouldering walls, teetering from too many pills, came into view. My grandmother died the same year my difficulties began. She'd been buried only three weeks when my spinal cord started ripping apart, three months by the time I was being wheeled into my first operating room, still with the impatience of the well, thinking vainly of scars and low-backed dresses. I had not properly mourned her, but I was not about to start right then, with my brain being squashed into crazy shapes.

For a few hours every evening, the spinal fluid

pumped less, a small grace period from the bursting compression inside my head the rest of the day. I'd make a dinner of steak and drink a half bottle of wine and then I would sit in the dining room and keep company while eating by talking to myself. Sometimes I'd pretend I was being interviewed. "Loneliness," I'd tell my interviewer, "is the most fleeting of emotions. It's just a tunnel you need to get through, and if you make it through, you can find yourself somewhere quite *sublime*, like atop a mountain." Other times I'd speak, brimming with generous wisdom, to friends who in the last year had disappeared in a miasma of transparent excuses: "I understand. You were so busy. You just didn't know how to deal." I'd convince myself of the power of these one-sided conversations to such an extent that I believed something about them was being transmitted. In Canada, ears were burning. Signals were felt. My husband and my father were looking into their Bloody Caesars with new understanding. After my meal, I'd have a nightcap of medical-marijuana spray and codeine with diazepam. I'd then listen to the Aaron Copland CD really, really loudly, thinking that my unseen neighbours would, from afar, admire my belief in the classic American dream. *Oh, Copland*, they'd whisper, getting up to gaze at the mountains that make such good sense with that music.

MOST DAYS. I busied myself with small, repetitive, contained tasks: folding and refolding my few T-shirts,
arranging my comb and soap on one side of the sink
and then putting them on the other side, wiping the
table before my breakfast and again after it. I'd been
annexed by the idea of keeping the house as neat as I'd
found it, as if its owner could pop up at any moment
from under the floorboards for a quick survey of its
state.

I also spent a good deal of time in the shower. I liked
showering because it felt progressive—a thing a normal person does before actually *leaving* a house—until
the day I found that I was screaming, and quite loudly,
under the water's spray. I caught myself mid-action,
although it seemed barely an action, more an incidental
practice, like twirling your hair while you're reading or
tapping the steering wheel when stopped at a red light.

I removed myself from the bathroom wrapped
in one of the house's extremely large white towels. I
forced my brain and my feet into a temporary peace
pact, an entente that would last at least long enough to
get me past the verandah. I had been in California for
two weeks. The plan had not been to fly to the other
side of the continent and act like a lunatic shut-in. The
plan had been more along the lines of the Resurrection.

Outside, my feet were on a carpet of pine needles
and dry brown earth, and my soles didn't know the

difference. It was like I was lugging myself around on medieval chopines, or those stilted geisha thongs, inches above the ground. I went as far as the storybook tree in the garden and sat on its bench. The tree was so old, its trunk so knobbly, it had an almost eccentric look to it. I let the towel I was wearing droop and my stitched back touch the corrugated bark of the oak. It was a California oak. I knew this because my grandmother had a tree in the back of her Palm Springs condo and she called it My Banyan Tree. One day her cleaning woman told her it was not a banyan, it was a California oak. My grandmother continued calling the tree her Banyan.

I surveyed the thirsty-looking earth. Near the tree was a patch of stalky flowers, skin-coloured things with thick stems, almost grotesque. Ojai has that smell that you can find only in the hottest and driest parts of America, a soapy deserty sagey smell, entirely mould-less, what might be the healthiest-smelling smell in the world. Leaning into these flowers offended that in an instant. I wondered if plants with such a harlot's-panty aroma could possibly be indigenous.

I padded to the field at the opposite end of the property to inspect the ground there. I measured the distance in past life, *belle vie* terms: the equivalent to one downtown Montreal block in pinching platform stiletto sandals after a seriously abusive all-nighter.

I stood at the edge of the field. It had a trampled look

to it, its covering a bramble of pine debris and earth balled into tarry mud pebbles. I pushed at a mud ball with one of my toes. It flattened satisfyingly into a disc. Holding my towel around me, I walked a couple of metres, watching my feet hitting the earth, squashing pebbles into discs, pebbles into discs. I felt something move in the corner of my eye and looked up to find the entire field streaming away from me. It was not just one brush-coloured rabbit but dozens of them, maybe hundreds. Stealth bunnies—bounding and twitching everywhere.

Panicked, I dropped the towel and left it on the field. The circles of tar on the soles of my feet were rabbit shit. I tottered in the direction of the orchard behind the house, where I'd noticed a garden hose looped through the white pickets, only to see a rat perched in profile on the fence, its rat's tail sticking straight out. It was enough. I was naked, limping, and who knew what other wildness lurked on this property? Just the night before, I had been watching the mountains change colour from the dining room windows when a bird flew straight into the glass, splatting dead on the stone verandah. I hadn't gone out to sweep it up, but now, entering the house through the dining room doors, I saw that the bird was gone, without a single smear on the stones. I was sure that the bird had not been a dream, but there was no way

I could be sure. I had not been keeping a diary. The only things I'd penned in days had been food lists and doodles, and one stoned midnight note that I'd found which read "FUCK YOU MOTHERFUCKERS," which I have no memory of writing.

I HAD ONCE asked my grandmother, who spent twenty-three out of twenty-four hours of every day alone on a bed clustered with television remote controls and transistor radios and copies of *TV Guide*, why she bothered with her trip to Palm Springs every year if she barely went out of the condo when she got there. She didn't play cards with the ladies at the pool and she didn't like the couples who went for earlybird specials and "to die for" desserts in someone's big white four-door. She was usually recovering from one surgery or another, being cantankerous or snooty to the unlucky person sent in to care for her. Her reply to my question was that she felt different in California, and that that was *interesting* to her. I held on to this answer because it was a rare sign of introspection in my grandmother. Even as a teen-ager, I wondered about what went on in her head, what her thoughts went *into*. She had no hobbies besides watching TV. She didn't do her own housekeeping. She didn't read; she never lasted with crafts. I used to swipe drugs from her bedside to use as comedown pills after club nights on coke and ecstasy, the joke being that my grandmother's medicines were strong enough to pummel any street drug. Once, alone in my bedroom, I tried a neat double dose of her medications to see if one could possibly grow wings from the pills in those prescription bottles. Maybe my grandmother's stonedness contained secret depths? But I just blacked out, waking up in my jeans the next morning with my lips glued whitely together.

The week after she died, I volunteered to clean out her Montreal apartment because my father was too broken up to do it. She left behind a mountain of junk. Mystery groupings of things: one thousand swizzle sticks; four cribbage boards; two decades' worth of Red Cross greeting cards; shopping bags filled with insoles or balls of synthetic yarn; piles of jewellery bought from infomercials. There wasn't a diary or a letter in my grandmother's hand. There wasn't an idea on a napkin or a line in a matchbook. There wasn't a further word as to how she endured. Under her bathroom sink, behind the boxes of Fleet enemas and several sad flaking hairbrushes, and a secret ashtray that we all knew about, I found a stack of filled-in crossword digests, the easy kind that you can buy in an airport before your flight. I remembered my grandmother in the airport, crabbily directing the person pushing her wheelchair. She wanted some candy. A crossword. It was incredible that these were the only proof that my grandmother was a woman with handwriting. I threw them all away, along with everything else, including the metal filing cabinet packed with claims and records from clinics bearing names like the Desert Medical Center. I did it with no remorse, dumping fast, as if a spirit could live in any old thing, as if the best I could do for myself was get out cleanly and quickly.

THE DAY AFTER the bunny event, I spent most of the morning lying on the sofa in the living room, the house's deepest middle. Whether the force rooting me there was physiological or psychological was impossible to know. My brain was a sizzling skillet, frying synapses like tiny shrivelling smelts. It was best to keep my eyes on the most inert things. On the ceiling, the central beam of the house ran parallel to my body. It was a nice beam; solid, dark oak. When the afternoon sun sent horizontal light into the living room, it revealed a long, almost elegant crack in the wood. I let my eyes follow the fissure. I stayed with it as it navigated knot and whorl until it reached the spot just above my head, where I saw what looked like an inscription. I got onto my knees and, steadying myself on the sofa back until a head rush cleared, saw that, no, this was not some primitive love scraping, the kind of thing you find filed into a tree. It may have been a stamp of some sort. Maybe a craftsman's marking.

I went to the drawer in the kitchen where I'd noticed before the pair of mini binoculars. I focused the lenses and saw that there were two boxes of text. They were hand-carved and exquisitely executed in a squared-off, barely serifed lettering, and framed by graphic, trumpet-shaped flowers and twining branches and vines. The first said:

THIS
IS
NOT
A
BEAM!

And the second, just as ornate:

MAY
WALLACE
OJAI
1935

The "M" in "May" and the "1" in "1935" shared the same long vertical line, making me unsure as to whether the person who'd carved this had done so in May 1935, or if the linking was only decorative, which would make

"May Wallace" the signature, a woman's name. Lacking my laptop, I could only speculate. I might have been satisfied with "This is not a beam" as some builder's joke if the carving wasn't so beautiful and, in 1935, fashionably whimsical: Magritte's pipe transposed onto a bungalow's beam in the wilds of California. That connection excited me—*Ceci n'est pas une pipe*; this is not what you think—it explained a vibe that could be sensed in the house, coming up from between the perfect drywall and new floorboards, a seep of something scintillant but patched over.

I gave my curiosity time to settle, and when it didn't, I located the phone book and found that Ojai did have a public library, and that it was less than a quarter of a mile away, in town. The idea of walking to an actual library in a genuine town that would contain real people landed like an epiphanic vision. I did not want to take a cab. I didn't want to explain to any driver why I needed a car for the distance most eighty-year-olds could walk in a footloose ten minutes. I also didn't want the connection between me and my purpose sullied. I trained for two days, walking slow laps along Mountainview. I found a good branch by the side of the road that I used as a walking stick. When I finally started into town, my feet didn't feel like wooden flippers anymore, more like jelly in socks of pins and needles. It had occurred to me that this was not necessarily *better*, but moving down the mountain, it did feel like progress.

OJAI'S TOWN CENTRE surprised me by being not at all like Palm Springs'. Palm Springs had that resort-town peculiarity of being a magnet for both the very aged and the very gay. Ojai seemed more homogenous — full of people who cycled in head-to-toe cycling outfits and said boomerish things like "Let's take a java break" and "Sixty is the new fifteen," referring, with much double entendre, to sunscreen. There were some faux pueblo buildings, and many in that Californian Mex-icasa style with the red tiles, but there were also hints of genteel Anglicism: wood filigree and small gardens of lavender; stained glass on the side of a tea house with tablecloths in chintz. My grandmother would never have gone to a place like that. In Palm Springs, once in a while she took me to an old deli on Indian Canyon called the Gaiety, which had pastel murals of highly erect cacti and eighty-five-year-old Litvak owners who, trust me, had *no idea*.

The library was made up of two low, butter-coloured buildings aproned by a courtyard full of yuccas and Saint Catherine's lace. I admired the garden for a minute, lean-ing idly on my stick and fancying what it would be like to be a local; just a native using the local library. I had a quiet feeling, the kind you get when you are about to enter a magnificent cathedral; you steel yourself for an upsurge of spirit.

Inside the library it was dry and comfortable, with

plain wood tables and padded chairs in worn eighties office shades of rose and teal. There were only two people in the main room: an old man in a bolo tie and slippers squinting at the Ventura County newspaper, and the librarian pushing a book cart.

"Can I help you?" she asked from behind her cart.

I wasn't sure how to go about this May Wallace business. I'd begun to question whether I'd imagined the carving in the beam. I felt weirdly transparent. My teeth felt transparent. My legs were dissolving. "I'm looking for information," I said. I could see my bangs separating at my eyelids, hairs shivering. I had no idea how I was coming across to this woman. Minutes before, approaching the glass doors of the library, I'd seen my reflection and thought, "Hey, that old lady is wearing the same striped T-shirt as me. I wonder if she also got it in . . . *Oh*. Right."

The librarian dipped her neck to catch my eyes. "What kind of information?" she asked. She was wearing a T-shirt too. It read: *Ojai Poetry Festival: Sounding the Conch*. She spoke so gently it could only mean that I looked like I should be in hospital, or in some kind of home, or at the very least lying down.

"Well, I'm writing a history of Ojai," I said, the first thing I could think of. "Maybe you won't have what I'm looking for." The librarian asked me if I planned on beginning with the Native Americans, and feeling so far from anything I actually needed, a fool on an idiot's quest, I said that I'd find my own way around. "Okay," she said. "Don't get lost on us now."

The stacks contained the sort of strangely balanced collection that might come by inheritance of dead people's libraries rather than any great financial endowment: paperbacks, bestsellers in dust covers, suddenly a huge expanse on birds here, a section on Romania there, and evidence that at least three donors were really into Carl Jung. I found the Art area and, expecting little, looked down for "W."

> May Wallace, *The Pot at the End of the Rainbow: An Ojai Memoir*
> Wallace, *I'm Astonished! A Memoir*
> May Wallace, *The Pottery of Love*
> Krishnamurti, Wallace, *Conversations with My Guru*
> Jiesen Edwards, *Radiant Palms: A Biography of May Wallace*
> Dennis, *American Dada Ceramics*

The librarian passed by again, pushing her trolley. "Sorry," I said, "but do you know anything about this May Wallace?"

"Well, sure. Everyone around here knows a little about May," she said. "She's a famous artist. She lived just up the hill on Mountainview. Are you looking for stuff on her?"

The librarian motioned for me to come to her desk. "She only died a couple of years ago. The whole town went to her funeral." Installing herself at her computer, the librarian said that, in addition to Wallace's published books, the library was also in possession of Wallace's private papers and handwritten diaries. It would be a few months until it was all organized enough to send off.

"Where's it going?" I asked.

"The Smithsonian," she said, her face beaming in the light of her monitor. "But right now it's all in the resource room in the back. You interested in seeing it?" I nodded and the librarian seemed genuinely pleased. "I'll sit you in the resource room, and you can have a look at everything nice and quiet. Now, I'll need to see a card, do you have a card?"

I gave her one of my old business cards, from a well-known magazine. I still kept a few in my wallet for status emergencies. "Nope," she said, pushing it back across the table. "I meant a library card. We'll need to get you a library card. Do you have an Ojai address?"

"It's 115 Mountainview."

"Oh, so you are in May Wallace's old house! Oh my goodness!" said the librarian. "Tell Beth Dooney I say hi. Is she still remodelling?"

I SPENT WHAT must have been several hours at the back of the library, immersed in May Wallace's papers and books, all of it like pages out of a bohemian fairy tale. Wallace was among the first to follow the guru Krishnamurti when he moved west. She had a Whartonian New York family whom she passionately despised, a lucky inheritance that came early, and a certain aesthetic ease in re-establishing herself in Ojai as a potter—a woman open-legged at the wheel in twin turquoise cuffs and great Kahloesque circle skirts. For a time, her studio was in the dining room of her house. She described the pink of the Topa Topas exactly as I saw them from the windows.

The more I read, the more furious I became with Beth Dooney. What kind of person buys a house that could be transported *whole* to the Smithsonian and then decides to whitewash the lot, fill it with a ton of generic New Horizonism, and then abandon it to take up some depressingly middle-aged female *villegiatura* in Italy? It was entirely possible that her neurotic drywall had been standing between me and something approaching fate. Who knows what could have been inscribed on more reachable posts before the renovators arrived?

There were lots of pictures of May Wallace in and around the house, which she had packed with Navajo rugs, pictures floor to ceiling, and cushion-festooned rattan. The place seemed to operate as a luxuriant way station for passing fascinating people. There was a frilly-edged photo of Wallace breakfasting on the verandah in a kimono with a man who is definitely Dali and a woman who looks a lot like Anaïs Nin, and another of her coyly hugging the California oak while being hugged by Edgar Varese, who is identified on the picture's back. The most striking photograph I found was one of Wallace and a different man, both of them draped like ancient Greeks for a costume party, and tented under a massive, sparkling night sky. It bore an inscription on its front, written in silvery ink with music hall humour: *Dearest May! I'll never forget the starry skies of "Oh, Hi!" Love, Double A.*

I rested my forehead on my arm and listened to my heart shush. Books and papers and pictures surged out across the table. I hadn't actually made great progress in getting through everything, but with this single picture bearing these two A's, I had found what I needed. I could have sought proof with a bit more foraging, a mention of Aaron Copland by full name, but had come up against an almost transcendental exhaustion. I packed my bag and, pretending I had no idea what I was doing, slipped the "Double A" photo in with my own things, and then one of May Wallace's handwritten diaries, too.

In the taxi back to the house, the cab swinging up the mountain under a sky like glitter-sprinkled velvet, I had the rare feeling that where I was and where

I was supposed to be had merged. If I had suffered an ever-widening gulf between me and my best destiny, I could now feel the gap coming together, almost by magnetic force. There are no meaningless coincidences, I thought. I had zero guilt about my pilfering. I was sure that everything that was happening—that had happened—was part of a pattern, that something was happening *through* me, and happening for a reason, and it felt enveloping enough to contain the whole Ojai night—the stars under my skin, the moon glowing from inside my rib cage.

THE NEXT MORNING, I sat under the oak tree, reading. May's handwriting was spiky and highly capitalized, the writing of a woman penning only ultimates. I'd scored well with the diary I'd stolen:

Aug 20, '46. They say it is the "Hottest August On Record." The ferocious heat made staying anywhere inside the House Intolerable. Night was welcome. As the Topas blushed pink, "AA" and I Made Love in the Garden, by the Tuberoses and carried their scent with us for the rest of the evening. The most Divine scent on Earth. L and K dined with us. L asked, "What perfume are you wearing?"...A Delicious Secret!

I crouched to examine those skin-coloured flowers. I pulled one up by the stalk and inhaled its flower-bomb outrageousness. I carried the tuberose back to the house. From the dining room windows, the mountains were flashing pink and I took the fact as an opportunity. I sucked a few long drafts of my marijuana spray, the smell of the tuberose impregnating the mist. I put the tuberose under my left bra cup, over my heart, and, propelled by a sense of a big looming *yes* of the life-changing sort, didn't care if I was acting like some nutso waif out of D. H. Lawrence. I put on *Appalachian Spring*, pulled a sofa cushion onto the dining room floor, and lay with it under my shoulder blades so that I could hang my head off it. Since the trip to the library, it was best to have nothing pressing against my skull.

I opened May's diary to the page where she and Double A do it, and placed the Copland photo in its seam. I then flipped the book over and laid it across my chest, like a little house, and closed my eyes. I did not know how to meditate. I was thinking, rather, of osmosis, of *absorption*. I concentrated on vibrations. The bass was in the floorboards. The windows were open, and I heard the crunch of gravel outside, the patter of feet, but was not afraid of wildlife coming in.

My husband didn't use the knocker on the front door. He just walked right in. "Hi," he said. "Um, are you sleeping?"

The voice was coming from behind my head. I lifted the diary off my chest as my husband bent down to meet me. The pores on his nose were the size of tea saucers.

"No one could reach you," he said, "and me and your father discussed it and—"

"How did you get here?" I asked, not knowing what else to say to this impossible vision.

"I flew," he said. "How else? I took a morning flight."

I was afraid to speak. The words were coming out and hanging in the air like a bizarre holiday garland. I wanted to stand up. I wanted to get the tuberose out of my bra.

"Are you stoned?" asked my husband, inspecting my eyes. He looked around and frowned. "Cowboy music?" he asked, heading to the stereo, turning the volume down, sniffing the air, wrinkling his nose. "You know," he said, "it kind of stinks in here."

FORTY-EIGHT HOURS LATER. I was back in my brick house in Montreal. Only hours after my husband arrived, the pain lining my brain had turned too much. I had to make him strip the bed of everything but its fitted sheet so that I could sprawl flat on my stomach with nothing touching me, my nose bearing into the mattress. He didn't like seeing me so still and silent, like a corpse in a pool. He took a side table out of the living room, brought it into the bedroom, put the television on it, and laid the remote by my bedside. He left the TV on all night in my room while he slept on the couch. He packed my things, and when it was time to leave, he carried me to the car, his arms under my shoulders and knees. "We'll get you a wheelchair at the airport," he said.

On the darkening drive to LAX, I told him about the day with the brown bunnies and I told him about Beth Dooney. My husband just drove, silent. "Did you pack the diary?" I asked. I hadn't said anything about May Wallace. I didn't have the energy for my husband's indifference. He nodded, not listening, but then caught himself. "Actually, no," he said. "You mean that hand-written thing? I put it with the other books. In the house. It didn't look like it was yours."

The weight of anticlimax was heavy on my eyelids; I watched the black-and-silver California sky tenting the highway, a sky that would soon be lost to me. My chronically sick grandmother died; I became chronic-ally ill: this would be my story, a plain one. I would live in a brick house in Montreal, and paradise would dwell beyond my personal horizon. My husband and I sel-dom spoke of Ojai after we'd left it, a chapter extracted. I still occasionally wonder if that diary stayed in that house, or if it made it to the Smithsonian, or got lost in the shuffle of Ojai real estate. Now and then I picture a lovely young biographer in a Washington library. She notices that in all of May Wallace's passionately documented days, a block of time is missing, and for the life of her, she can't imagine where it may have gone.

CHAMP DE MARS

ELLEN WOLKE WAS THE shape of an apple, round and
enormous. She had been heavy for years—and every
year it surprised her, the way it surprises a person to
learn that they graduated forty years ago, not ten. Still,
she knew it to be different now, because when she ate,
people watched. People used to look at Ellen for other
reasons, this wispy woman, with long, rib-skimming
hair the colour of red milky tea. Now it was only: How
does such size happen? (Or if they knew Ellen: yes,
that's how that size happens.)

Not long ago, Ellen counted the number of times
she'd eaten in one day: fourteen. That was more than
usual, and half of it was blind eating, emotional eating.
She counted silently, tapping her fingers on a placemat
with a plate of plum cake on it and a half-drunk glass

of milk. Dory was sitting across from her, with his own slice of cake, his glass of milk full. He was wearing his dress shirt buttoned up but without a tie, a purgatorial mode Ellen associated with architects and people who didn't dress themselves.

Dory was now both of those things. Although he'd always worn a tie before.

"You look Amish," she said, not really to Dory, and also not to May, who was making herself busy washing Ellen's cake pan, and was from the Philippines, and wouldn't know the Amish. In truth, Dory looked more retarded than anything, his eyes reverting to childhood, his features slowly, giddily capitulating.

Even a year ago, he had still been the old Dory, the real Dory, forgetful, but not so much that it turned his insides out: he couldn't remember the name of Ellen's place of work, the institute that she'd founded decades before — The Children's Place? The Children's Centre? It's the Learning Centre? Are you sure? Then he couldn't remember how to adjust his drafting table, then he didn't know where his fine-tip pens were.

When they were first married, forty-five years ago, Ellen used to accuse Dory of a hypervigilance that bordered on the obsessive. An architect is an architect, and a German architect, enough said, but still, it was something to get used to, something Ellen could only work around. All the fine-tip pens had to go in a certain narrow white ceramic cup. The cup needed to be in the upper left-hand corner of the desk. There were a million things like that. Dory used to say that when he was a youth, his head had always been in the clouds. He would lose a shoe on his way to school. He would become deaf when drawing pictures of fanciful mazes or crazy Christmas trees in class, the teacher repeating his name over and over: *Dorian, Dorian Wölke, bist du da?*

To become an integrated man of line and angle he had needed to train those tendencies out of himself. The fine-tip pens needed to be in the cup, said Dory, because if not, they would be in the bathroom, the bedroom, the fridge.

Ellen found pens in the fridge. She phoned the doctor. Dory's diagnosis was Alzheimer's. Early.

"Must we call it *early* when I am seventy-one years old?" asked Dory.

"You could have thirty years ahead of you," is what the doctor answered.

At first, it wasn't what Dory called the heart of his brain that was being affected, just the outer areas. Ellen sent Dory to buy canned artichokes and when he returned bewildered, saying he was unable to locate his reason for being in the supermarket, that he felt he was "half in a dream," Ellen's legs began to tremble, like the ground was shuddering under her feet.

"Well, I know that I still like artichokes, and fresh more than *canned*," said Dory defensively, as if having his tastes about him meant nothing could be too wrong.

Of course taste had always been a fortress for Dory. He was famous for a kind of rabble-rousing sternness — the sort that went over better internationally than at home. He often argued that his ideal building would be totally invisible, making his structures in gleaming glass as if it was a concession. Ellen met and married him while he was embroiled in the controversy over the last project he would ever undertake in Montreal, (from then on he would always favour work in Europe and Japan): the Champ de Mars metro station, 1967, a merciless glass box aboveground with expanses of glass wall underground, displaying monolithic rock face. The other stations were friendly affairs with bubbly orange plastic seating and op-art murals. Ellen still remembers watching her new husband on a small black-and-white television, sitting placidly in his chair as a critic in a psychedelic shirt called the station a mean, modernist throwback.

"Aha, but there cannot be such a thing as a modernist throwback," Dory corrected, his square face poreless as paper under the hot lights. "Only a modernist throw-now, or in a degenerate state, a modernist throw-forward. A train goes along a track, through an underground tunnel. There is a *sense* to be followed there. It is not orange plastic *blobbery*."

DORY'S SYMPTOMS WORSENED after the diagnosis. The doctor said this often happened — a letting go — although when Ellen described some of the examples of degeneration to the doctor, he said he could not comment on whether these were Alzheimer's symptoms or changes in aesthetic preference. Dory had eagled in on a very small tear in the low beige loveseat in his study, where for more than four decades he'd sat every morning to gather his thoughts. Dory wanted Ellen to fix the tear with a patch he'd found in the house — something from when their daughter, Sam, was a girl, heart-shaped, red gingham, insanely wrong for the subdued sable of his Italian loveseat.

The day prior, she'd found a greeting card propped up on Dory's drafting table, blank, as if waiting for inscription. On the front of the card was a photograph of a baby, sleeping in a flowerpot, wearing a costume hat that looked like a large daisy. Dory's standard stationery sat in stolid stacks nearby—the white stock with letterhead so light you needed full sunlight to see it properly: DORIAN WOLKE AND ASSOCIATES.

When Ellen asked Dory about the baby card, he looked at it as if he had never seen it before.

"Oh, isn't that sweet?" he said, bringing it close to his face, his narrow black glasses. "Remember when Sam was a baby, and she'd look up with those eyes?"

It wasn't usual, either, his pulling Sam into conversation, just like that. It was always better between them when they didn't speak of Sam.

Dory was still going to the office every day, a short walk from the house, but Ellen became anxious when seeing him go. He'd stopped talking about builds and articulations and elevations. He ambled out the door every morning with none of his normal velocity. And what if baby cards were infiltrating the office? All those tight, strict people.

It had occurred to Ellen to follow her husband, and one morning she got as far as the car in the driveway. Keys in the ignition, she talked herself down. Dory was just going to the office. If there was a real problem, Dory's partner Suskind would phone her. When Sam had begun cutting school, leaving the house in that same unbusy way, there had been a call from the school soon enough. *How was Samantha's mononucleosis?*

But Suskind didn't call, so Ellen phoned him. His silences were long. He said Dory was coming in late and taking unusually long lunches. Otherwise, he said Dory looked to be keeping very busy, drafting in his office for hours.

"Oh, so he has a new project?" asked Ellen.

"It seems more like doodles," said Suskind. "Personal stuff."

Ellen vaguely said that Dorian was taking medication.

"He made a very intricate drawing of a dollhouse for a junior partner's eight-year-old daughter," continued Suskind, who, after so many decades, still had no name on Dory's intractable letterhead.

A few times, Ellen had caught herself counting backwards, dazedly tapping a table or chair or steering wheel: 2014, 2004, 1994, minus 2 = 22 years. She had reached the point where her old pain was such a familiar padding, she was able to feel it in a way that didn't cause immediate suffering. For years there would barely be a day when she didn't have a minutes-long freeze-out moment, standing stock-still in some hallway, overcome by everything she was holding down.

But with all this Dory stuff, past reactions were returning, storylines coming back. Sam's "mononucleosis" had been hooky on a grand scale. Ellen watched her current students, with their pinging phones, and thought about how it would be impossible to disappear as effectively as back when Sam started skipping class to ride the metros all day. Now, the child would come home and the parent could say, *I couldn't reach you*, and begin their investigation.

Back in 1992, Sam could do more of what she wanted, and what she wanted was to experience the connections between metro lines; to see whether she could travel through every intersection, from every possible direction, within a certain time frame. The mission had taken on some edge of urgency.

"And every day you're doing this metro thing alone, Sam?"

"Well, Mom, it's not exactly a group activity."

This type of quirky experimentation wasn't unusual. Sam went on these trips: spans of not eating meat, or boycotting any but primary colours, or only taking down class notes in code. Once she decided not to speak for a week. She walked around with a notebook opened to a page on which she had written *I have taken a vow of silence. Thank you for your understanding.* Dory had always been enchanted by these eccentricities. At dinner parties, he would describe his daughter's stints, roaring with laughter, while Ellen had to force herself not to make connections between her daughter and the type of behaviours she saw every day at the Learning Centre. After all, the Centre wasn't only for kids who had to wear helmets or couldn't be touched. It was also for the growing number of borderline cases, kids nearly functional, or just functional. Colleagues increasingly used the term "on the spectrum."

"Don't worry," Sam said, flinging her lanky legs

out in front of her, her undone shoelaces whipping her shins. "I am doing all my homework. I am just doing it *on the metro.*"

She would enter McGill the following year, at fifteen. The dean of the university, the brother-in-law of one of the architects at Dory's firm, came for coffee. Ellen, an excellent and prolific baker, offered plain cookies from a box. Sam went on some long, dazzling spiel about Montreal's concrete architecture, something she probably memorized — likely by accident — from one of the journals Dory often had stacked on the kitchen table. The dean was convinced, and Dory, who was set on getting Sam out of her wholly regular high school early, beamed at the done deal.

But Ellen knew it was trouble to put a teenager in university three years early. Sam didn't have an easy time with friends. And this metro thing gave Ellen a creepy feeling, like some gateway had opened, although into what, who knew.

Ellen also noticed that Sam had taken to fishing out old toys from the garage: a pony with a long pink mane you could brush; a sticker album with a sparse collection in it; a few cats, hearts, babies with pudgy faces in scalloped frames. Sam never cared for these things much as an actual child. She always showed more interest in maps, or indeed math, or making small, complicated universes of her own design. Once, when she was eight, she spent days creating an increasingly elaborate metro system that ran throughout her bedroom, ransacking Ellen's sewing basket for buttons and the pantry for chocolate chips and Dory's trash can for punched-out holes. Ellen and Dory tiptoed over the dozens of snaking dot-lines.

"Sam, dear, why does this metro line climb the wall?" asked Dory, lifting his glasses to closely examine a row of buttons taped straight up a wall, like a done-up shirt, ending at the window above Sam's bed.

"Well. *All* my train tracks are elevated," Sam explained in that bossy, know-it-all way that often annoyed Ellen. *"That,"* she said, pointing to the window, "is where they turn into *air tracks.*"

The night after they found out about Sam's absences, Dory took off his glasses and put them by his low bedside table and then got under the white sheets of the broad white bed he shared with Ellen. Scratching his brows, as if to free them of tics, he said he saw Sam's subway project as "exploration." Ellen wrenched the sheets off herself, and stood over the bed, her nightgown quivering, her arms crossed over her then-bony chest.

"Sam is clearly overwhelmed!" she said, half hoping that their daughter, down the hall with her twitching antenna ears, heard. There was no question McGill should be deferred. "And I don't care what strings the dean pulled! *I know my Sam!"*

"I just don't think we should coddle her for the sake of comfort," answered Dory, measuredly.

"Comfort can foster laziness," he continued, as if musing about one of his glass cubes.

Ellen watched her husband's square face, his mouth opening and closing with pompous stupid words, his small eyes nude and pathetic without their glasses, and she hated him and Sam at the same time, the two of them, with all their collusion — their big alien brains and cold-fish affection and long accordion-legs. Sam would miss stairs, curbs, and Dory would tell her that she needed to *think* her limbs into submission, the same way he had when he was her age. Head in the cloud and knees meet the ground, he would drill, while Ellen was reduced to flapping mother, dabbing with antiseptic.

"Ow! Leave me alone, Mom!"

"Yes, *leave* her already, Ellen."

The first semester at McGill was difficult. Sam didn't show up to classes. She called her art history professor "the pedophile," and her urban design class her "urban disaster" class. She refused breakfast in the morning, and at night wouldn't have anything but strawberry jam sandwiches and Perrier. One morning, she refused to get up and Dory physically lifted her out of her bed and plunked her in the hallway.

Ellen heard the strange bodily thud from the kitchen and ran upstairs to find her daughter lying like a corpse on the floor, her eyes closed, her arms crossed over a pink stuffed monkey that had come with her out of bed. Oddly, Ellen still remembers first thinking how unusual it was, that Dory and Sam had had this close contact, the house's two avowed "non-huggers," both of whom would flinch when embraced, even by her.

That was the beginning of that day: November 6, 1992.

The people in the Champ de Mars metro who later saw the tall girl with the backpack and loose shoelace step off the platform said they could not tell whether she had wanted to. She just looked like she wasn't thinking about what she was doing. "It was like the platform ended under her feet," said one woman, hoarse with tears, because she'd seen everything from just a metre away, the pink monkey blasting out of the girl's backpack on impact, "and her feet didn't notice."

FOR A WHILE. after that, Ellen had needed Dory out of the house. It looked bad, him leaving to save some European bank building in the month after Sam's death, but the truth was that Ellen wanted him away. She looked at him and all she saw was Sam, and all the instincts Ellen had ignored, because she couldn't manage to hurdle them over Dory's certainties.

The split lasted several months, Ellen deciding

eventually that even a Dory she found guilty was better than the new loneliness alone. During his absence,
Ellen could do nothing but bake, for hours, tears welling into her flour, her mixing bowls weirdly the same,
her cakes coming up impossibly the same, and every
single thing besides them floating off in all directions, in
some stark, over-clear atmosphere, air she didn't know.
Her skirts were increasingly too tight. At night, sleep
was distant. Ellen would close her eyes and imagine
putting her entire face in a big white cake with white
icing. She'd get out of bed, and go downstairs and bake
something more sensible — as if bran muffins or zuc-
chini bread were some normalizing force. It still makes
Ellen shudder in nearly intolerable shame, now, when
she recalls the night she ran out of most ingredients,
and the sun came up to reveal countertops crowded
with six hundred meringues, and Ellen still sweating
over the stove, as if catering an Easter wedding.

SOMEWHERE IN HERSELF, through all the years since,
Ellen thought that her pain, a pain that came to feel
sealed, but never healed (and all mothers who lose children know this, how the pain becomes like a hide you
get used to, but which is never useful, the way other
pains can be), would absolve her from future hardship.
She organized her continuing life around this belief.

She would never divorce, no matter how much love was lost. She would not become ill, no matter how fat she became. If Dory died, he'd die an old man, suddenly, in his sleep. Because the worst thing had already happened to her, and she'd absorbed the blow and remained upright. Surely, for this, some kind of immunity? Some reward?

The day Dory didn't show up at work, Suskind had waited until noon, and then phoned. Was Dorian with Ellen? No? Well, he was not at the office.

Ellen put on her coat, which billowed like a tent around her round waist in the city wind. She scoured the likeliest streets, trying not to miss a corner, a block, every hour explaining to Suskind from her cellphone that no, he should not be calling the police. In truth, she began wondering whether the police were needed. She was losing track of where she'd been, dizzy in her coat, her face mapped red with exploding blood vessels, and Dory was nowhere. She found herself outraged by her own worry. How long was the right amount of time to do this? She imagined waiting at home, in the kitchen, the kettle coming on. Eventually, Dory would return, or be returned.

Then she knew where to find him.

Before the city redesigned it, commuters had nicknamed Champ de Mars the Stone Aquarium, the Glass Coffin. And even with Dory's ingenious dehumidification techniques and innovative glazing, the windows showcasing the underground rock often wept with condensation. They were replaced with black granite. Ellen recalled how Dory railed that his station had been made to look like it was "coated in nouveau riche kitchen counter."

Walking to the station, an embedded shard shifted in Ellen's heart. She envisioned Dory, confused in his new way, with those too-bright eyes, on the platform, being roughly handled by security. He gains his old self too late, asking in his wrong-accented French, *Do you know who I am? I built this bloody station.*

Oui, oui, monsieur, of course you did.

Banishing the fantasy before she could dissect it — because something in her did relish it — Ellen paid for the metro, took the escalator underground, and, from the concrete mezzanine over the tracks, saw Dory. He was sitting on a bench, his back against the granite wall of the eastbound platform, his briefcase on his lap. He was using it as a desk. He seemed to be drawing.

With his glasses and fine pens, Dory still looked like himself, even while his metro station was nearly unrecognizable. He had been totally right about the new materials being wrong. Over time, the black granite had taken on strange stains. In the sections backing the platform benches, the stone had absorbed the heat and oils off the people sitting and waiting for the trains, making darker, human-shaped blobs appear in the granite. The Ghosts of Champ de Mars, people called them, not without superstition, because the station had by then gained a reputation for being jinxed, dark beyond its design flaws. They said you could feel those shadows on your back.

A security guard approached Ellen. She must have been there a while. Did Madame need help in knowing which train to take? Ellen pointed at Dory. She spoke with the overspecific voice she used with parents at the Learning Centre. She needed all her powers. "That man with the briefcase," she enunciated. "He is my husband. He is okay. He is an architect —"

"Oh, he's here all the time," said the guard, chuckling, motioning to Dory with his chin. "The guy who makes pictures. He draws like that for hours, and then he gives it away and leaves, like he's finished his day of work. Me? I've talked to him; hello and good day. I could tell he was an artist or something, not just a crazy —"

The guard suggested Ellen go back up the escalator, to see the woman who took tickets upstairs. Dory had given her one of the drawings. Nearing the glass ticket booth, Ellen was bothered that she couldn't remember if it had been part of Dory's original design. She'd have to get a longer view. If there was a certain amount of room on either side of it, then she'd know it was Dory's. His symmetry was to her predictable.

The ticket taker had a tan the colour of doll skin and pink nail polish, too thickly applied. She held up the page for Ellen, her spidery, fake-looking lashes blinking. Ellen wondered whether it was normal for women like this to take jobs in the metro. Maybe it was.

"It's nice, you know?" said the ticket taker, her voice crackly behind the booth's glass. "To have something that somebody really made?"

The drawing was Dory's, but unlike anything of Dory's Ellen had ever seen. It was a heart of unimaginable complexity — full of rooms, staircases, landings, elevations, a heart almost limitless in its tiny, line-drawn chambers. Ellen became breathless with ownership and irritation: this girl behind glass, with this loony valentine Ellen could barely comprehend as being related to her own life. She arranged her big coat about herself.

"How do I know that he really gave this to you?" said Ellen, more sharply than she'd wanted.

"Well, why would I make it up?" said the ticket taker. "Getting a picture from some guy who hangs around the metro drawing hearts all day?"

SOON DORY WAS forgetting basic things: where his clothes were kept, how to dial Ellen's cell number, how to eat a muffin still in its paper cup. He was home all the time. Ellen needed to place an ad for a caregiver. In fielding calls, Ellen felt a little bloom of relief, a warmish ember of freedom amid the grey exhaustion clouding her lower back. She could just leave for the Learning Centre five mornings a week. If she needed a haircut, she could just leave the house and get one. A nurse would stay with Dory. Ellen could just leave him. That would be fine.

All the caregivers were middle-aged Philippinas with springtime names: April and May and Vivian. When June Phan called, Ellen thought she was also a caregiver. June quickly corrected her. She had that irritating young person's habit of making every line sound like a question: "I'm, like, a reporter?"

"Dory!"

"I'm with the *McGill Daily*? The student paper?"

"Dory, pull the paper off the muffin — Dorian!"

"Should I call back?"

"No — Dorian, can you hear me? Paper off! A reporter. Okay. Yes?"

"I am doing a story. I mean I want to. About Dorian Wolke, I mean, your husband —"

It's a wonder Ellen didn't hang up then. The old Dory had hated journalists. He never gave the people writing about buildings any of his time. He used to call what they did "dancing about architecture," in other words, skirting the point. He always said the same thing: his buildings were entirely transparent. No interpretation required.

But June Phan had information. Did Mrs. Wolke know about Dory's drawing in the metro? She did? Well, did she know there were at least thirty of these drawings? Always hearts, always given to girls, usually college students, or, June suggested, girls who looked like students to Dory.

"And just so you know, like, I don't want you thinking I am going to make him look perverted for that —"

June began seeing Dory in the same week as May began working for Ellen — May, with her many depressing accessories: strings with clips so Dory could keep things around his neck; large-print checklists placed everywhere from bedside to toilet; plastic baskets for grouping stuff together; all things Ellen hadn't even come close to thinking of.

Watching June Phan remove her knit hat and fold her long, maroon-tinted hair over one shoulder, Ellen considered how death was simply the only way out now. It would be her death or it would be Dory's, and if it were hers, she might not mind that much. Dory used to say the way to deal with this type of feeling was to remove yourself from it. Look at it in hard light and say, oh, hello, idiotic emotion, you are not me, you are just an emotion. In Dory's view, there was no such thing as a person trapped by *feelings*. Position yourself correctly, and all the trouble in the world could just slide over you, water over rock.

In the kitchen, May was giving Dory applesauce.

"The applesauce is homemade," Ellen said to June, addled by the day-lit vision of Dory and his nurse — he with his shirt done all the way up under a red-striped bib, she in a tunic with an all-over teddy bear pattern.

"Oh, lucky Mr. Dory-Dory! You have a young girl visitor! A beautiful girl!"

June removed from her backpack two well-worn notebooks, a pile of photocopies, and a digital recorder.

Dory beamed at June from above his candy cane bib, an accidental Santa Claus, an avuncular uncle, a Werther's butterscotch chef with gleaming eyes.

"Will you be okay with everyone leaving the room?" June asked Dory directly.

Dory nodded, clearing his throat.

"Just, first, dear!" he said. "Can you please tell me and your mother why it took you so long to get here?"

USUALLY THE INTERVIEWS lasted twenty minutes. Ellen made a project of cleaning the basement, filling garbage bags for the charity truck, when June was with Dory. She had gotten as far as the room they always called the larder — a dry, windowless warren in the middle of the basement that she used as a second pantry. It was one of the few places in the house with no windows, its dry smell of old flour and paper bags of sugar never changing. Ellen found a bunch of dead meal moths on a shelf, disintegrating. She brushed the powdered wings and carcasses into her palm, and found she could hear June from where she stood. She now had the cadence of a teacher. "Can you talk about this heart you drew?" asked June.

"I made that?"

"You made it in Champ de Mars. Do you remember?"

"I know that place very well. Champ de Mars!"

"How do you feel about it? Do you miss your glass walls?"

"Oh, they won't be taking those down for some time yet."

"What do you mean?"

"Well, my dear, we are long before any of that mess."

"You think we are before? Like, we're in the 1990s? Sitting in this kitchen? Now?"

"Of course we are! After all, you are here, right?"

Ellen put down the open flour bag she was holding, flecked with moths like chocolate chips in batter. She clomped up the stairs and was soon pulling open her kitchen drawers and cupboards. The spoons, the bowls, the mixer, four black plums from the fridge.

"I am baking a cake," she announced, clattering her pans.

"What kind of cake?" asked June, above the din, as if this too was material.

"Plum, as you can see, from the plums," said Ellen, unkindly.

"But Ellen!" said Dory, standing up in the noise. "Sam doesn't like plum cake. She likes chocolate cake. Chocolate cake with cream cheese icing!"

Ellen looked at the counter, June at her tape recorder.

"Sam doesn't like plum cake," Dory said again. "She likes chocolate cake with cream cheese icing. So why don't you make us some chocolate cake, then?"

As Ellen ushered June out of the house, apologizing firmly, she didn't know that June's newspaper article would lead to many more like it, like one dagger after another, all of them framing Dory's decline in the same feel-good way. The *New York Times* called her husband's dementia "a historic creative awakening," this man who made so many glass boxes back in the twentieth century.

June Phan will move to New York for an internship, and before she leaves she will call Ellen and say she would like to come and say goodbye to Dory. On that day, Ellen will hide his diapers and his wheelchair and his cans of protein drink, and wait with the kettle on, listening for the doorbell, as if something in its ringing might awake another beginning, or at least an end, but the girl will forget, and never come.

SHALOM ISRAEL!

AFTER MY HUSBAND LEFT. I really didn't mind the quiet.
There is a guilty static that builds up in the spaces
where a couple's come apart, and it was a relief to be
free of it. At night, I slept with my bedroom window
open, feeling the blue mineral air come in like an un-
furling ribbon. In the mornings, I would open the curtains or look up from my teacup and wonder what was
going to come next. The person who conquers illness
asks: Am I now saved or do I still need saving? Time
felt open and luxurious, a plane ripe for development.
I knew, somehow, that something good was going to
happen. Then my mother moved in.

My mother moved in with me. She'd sold her square,
sound house of forty years. She said she needed some
time to figure out where she'd live next. I didn't ask why

she didn't think this through before putting the old house up, before accepting an offer, before packing her decades up, and sending everything into storage. Sometimes you have to do things in a certain way for reasons that don't withstand explanation.

At any rate, I couldn't tell her no. A mother does not raise a child to be turned away from her door, valise in hand, at sixty. And I was after all idle, greeting my dawning survivor status with a remnant delicacy, nudging around a large house in my bathrobe. Plus, there was something going on with my mother. She seemed like a woman who was giving herself trouble, experiencing some kind of welling up that was rupturing a system that had always worked for her before.

For starters, she was exercising too much, more than her normal regimen—she was now counting steps, and putting a good deal of faith in various weights and scales for measure, trying to outrun the unacceptable truth that at sixty her body magic was flattening, the space that once contained so much hard wonder was now filling with lumpier problem material. There were daily injuries: a frozen shoulder, an inflamed knee, a cold flash emanating from her hip, a broiling poker at a neck nerve. She liked to say these were old dance grievances, turning what in anyone else would be a symptom of age into a reminder of beautiful youth. A few times I saw her examining herself in my hall mirror, smoothing her sweater down and sideways over her hips, looking for some remembered effect. She'd once made me press her belly so that I could understand what she'd convinced herself of at the YMHA that day: "You see?" she'd said, bearing down, holding her breath. "It's all muscle. Just a little fat on top. What makes it thick is the muscle."

BACK WHEN I was afraid that my sickbed was growing pink padded sides and a cover, I asked my mother what she thought happened after death. In my faltering state, I had decided that my own feeling was that what happened was conditional on your disposal. If you were buried, you became earth. If you were sunk at sea, you became shark food.

My mother fished for her car keys in her purse. "So you become a shark?" she asked.

"Until it shits you out. Then you become sand—"

"This is stupid," said my mother, who finished the conversation by telling me that she couldn't imagine a time when she was not or would not be *her*.

"Even before you were born?"

"I don't know," said my mother. "I have tennis."

WHEN SHE MOVED in, her effect on my house was explosive and immediate. She fired the maid because she said she didn't like some extra body around the place all the time. She claimed the guest room with a detonation of clothes inside out on the floor and newspapers in Hebrew and open tubes of lipstick and spilling bottles of jojoba oil and the straps and bands that are the effluvium of the contemporary fitness nut. She filled the fridge with beige tubs of eggplant in various states of purée. She left whatever novel she was reading face down in front of the toilet. Lately this was one by a famous Israeli writer, a tragic tale about losing a child to war. I knew about the writer: in an excruciating turn, one that for a split second obliterates all rational ideas about the limits of parental influence, he'd lost his own son in Lebanon while writing the book.

My mother and I were, at first, shocked at the happiness of our living arrangement. Perhaps afraid to rock our unlikely ark, we watched hours of television together, camping out in the carpeted den that used to be my husband's warren, sometimes with sandwiches on our knees, as delighted as young girls getting away with something. We watched all of the dance competition shows, my mother telling me which dancers had real training, and which had no chance.

"This dancer is disgusting," she'd said of one.

"She's not disgusting, she's just a little heavy."

"She looks fat like an elephant," said my mother.

"Mom, stop it, be nice."

"What nice? She's on*stage*."

On one of the local channels, there was a commercial for the upcoming season of shows at Place des Arts, including a nostalgic song-and-dance stage spectacle for Israel's sixtieth birthday entitled *Shalom Israel!* I looked it up on the Internet. The show was created by the Israeli choreographer Ronen Chen, and on tour, it was stopping in Montreal for one night only. For my mother, it was major. My mother called Chen "the man of my career." He was the one who had discovered her some forty-five years earlier on a Tel Aviv beach, grabbing her by her ponytail and telling her about auditions. My mother knew all the performers in the *Shalom Israel!* show. When the Place des Arts commercial came on again, she pointed at the television mutely, bottlenecked by so much lifestuff coming up.

A few days later, my mother came into the kitchen dressed in exercise clothes.

"I am making a power walk to the box office," she announced, putting her leg up on a chair to fasten the Velcro on an ankle weight.

"What box office?"

"At Place des Arts. I want for us tickets for the Israel show."

"Isn't that a bit far to walk?" I asked. "It's the other side of the city."

"Don't worry," said my mother, zipping up a leather fanny pack, ignoring my words about slippery sidewalk sleet and too many kilometres. "I'm going to buy the cheapest tickets for the show."

Buying the cheapest tickets was my mother's favourite trick. Pay for a nosebleed seat and then move to a better one that had remained vacant after the show's start.

"You know last year I sat in the front row for *The Barber of Seville* for fifteen dollars," said my mother.

"*The Barber of Seville* didn't have an audience filled with other Israelis planning on doing exactly the same thing."

"So? We'll be more quick," said my mother, forgetting my slowness, my story, the wheelchair folded in the coat closet, still too fresh from use to give away just yet.

LATER THAT AFTERNOON. I found my mother sitting in the kitchen with her ankle weights loose on the table along with a ticket envelope from Place des Arts. I looked at the tickets (X48 and X46). My mother was staring out the window, her face ashen. It was a gloomy northy 5 p.m., cold and salt grey. My mother was holding a heating pad to her right shoulder and a bag of frozen peas to her left knee. She actually looked rueful. I stood awkward in the kitchen doorway, unused to seeing her like this—what was it? Melancholy? Something having to do with thinking and feeling at the same time. She usually moved too fast for that sort of thing.

"Did you get good tickets for the show?" I asked.

"No," she said, her voice like a puddle.

"Well, I'm excited," I said, lying.

My mother shrugged, then winced, her shoulder. "For you it's normal to be in the audience."

"You know, if you hadn't moved to Canada, you'd be onstage in the show for sure —" I said. I put on a waxy announcer's voice: "'And now, presenting the star of Shalom Israel 2009! The lovely...'"

"Of course I would," said my mother, fussing with her heating pad. "This is not a question that I would."

"Then there's nothing to regret."

"I don't *regret*. I don't like talking about this."

"About the past?"

"It's already finished. There is nothing to talk about."

MY MOTHER WAS never a fan of memory in general. Of her past, she relayed little to me as a child. Where she'd come from; where she'd been. I knew only a toy history, a jack-in-the-box phoenix-from-ashes: how she'd been saved from a trap of filthy poverty by her body's physical brilliance; how at the stroke of sixteen her dancing had freed her from her mother's cruel and unhealthy apartment.

Not surprisingly, my mother had never been any good at keeping photos properly. In the basement of her house she'd had only a couple of coming-apart shoeboxes stuffed with a disarray of decades: frilly-edged colour shots of her as a Tel Aviv beach babe stuck on the back of ancient black-and-whites of shocked-looking people off a boat from Russia; me at six, toothless and grinning in a red snowsuit, hanging by a loop of dry tape to a picture of my mother as my father's bride, her hair freshly cut for her Canadian wedding into a curled-under pudding-bowl style.

Over the years, I had taken a few of the pictures I liked most from my mother's neglected stash, making small ordered collections for myself. "I want to show you something," I now said, leaving the kitchen for the oak cupboard in the hall, taking a string-tied packet from a drawer and rushing back to the table before my mother lost interest.

It was a series of pictures of my mother in a black leotard and a high ponytail on the sand, probably promotional shots. She is such a knockout in the photos, I used to keep one in my wallet, to impress upon a certain sort of boyfriend just what kind of genetic pool they were dealing with.

"Look at my waist!" said my mother, shuffling through the black-and-white photographs, nodding at her figure. She then stopped to peel off a small coloured snapshot stuck to one of the leotard pictures. "This one is something different," she said. "This is a different time. This is not in Tel Aviv. This is Miami."

On inspection it looked like Miami, my mother reclining poolside on a chair made of orange plastic spaghettis, pecan-brown in a yellow knit bikini, her metres of hair rolled atop her head in a bun the size of an American car turbine. She's staring straight at the camera and lying next to a man who is looking at her. His hair is brushed back into a small bouffant. He wears short trunks.

"This is Ronen Chen," said my mother, taking the photo and holding it in front of her face, her eyes round past the picture's edges. "This is in Miami. This is when we were in Miami."

I nodded. I wondered if my mother knew that I knew about the time this picture was taken. I knew about my mother and Ronen Chen in Miami. The Miami story was related to me by my mother's sister in Tel Aviv, offered in consolation one weepy afternoon during a teenaged summer of lovesickness, boys coming and going, waves crashing on the beach. Before flying back to Canada, I had asked my aunt for the story two more times, my own heart pain mitigated by the story of my mother's.

The story takes place during the last section of a six-month world tour. Ronen Chen had by then asked my mother to marry him. She had said no. Her life was only just beginning. Inside herself, she believed there would be many other loves like Ronen Chen.

The dancers were painting a thick stripe along the North American East Coast, beginning in Montreal, where the newspapers called the Chen Israeli Folkloric Dance Troupe peace ambassadors from a country at war, and raved about the barefoot lead dancer with the ponytail that grazed the deeply curved small of her back.

My father had been only one of her backstage courtiers in the city. She accepted his invitation for a late dinner on a whim. Nerdy and awkward, having read books on dating etiquette, he took her out for steak Diane in a dark French restaurant downtown. He urged that they drink a strong drink before the meal and after the meal a sweet liqueur. Between those, he ordered a bottle of red wine for just the two of them. My mother was unused to liquor and I imagine my father confused my mother's fine bone structure with experience. Had he known of her deep virginity, he likely would not have pressed on to her hotel.

THE TROUPE'S TOUR continued for many weeks. Quebec City, Ottawa, and Toronto whizzed by, the dancers more exhilarated with every sold-out show. But after a two-week stint in New York City, my mother felt uncommonly spent. By Washington, DC, she was skipping the after-show receptions in the homes of Outstanding Members of the American Jewish Community for early nights. In Richmond, the troupe stayed in a plaster-columned hotel called the Dixie Motor Lodge, and my mother suffered from nausea from the ham and the milky-white gravy on the breakfast plates.

Miami was the tour's last stop, and there was a day-long break before the final shows began. The troupe was put up in a high, white resort hotel that curved around a swimming pool which was the shape of a perfect circle. In the morning, my mother and Chen sat poolside. Instead of the usual aqua, the bottom and sides of the pool were painted a dark blue, which created a mysterious, lakelike effect that made my mother uncomfortable. When Chen jumped in to cool off, my mother gasped, for a moment believing he might never re-emerge.

Chen had just told my mother that he wanted her to do an extra solo in the Miami shows, something special for the tour's finale. "No, no, the other dancers will be jealous," she said, just to say something. Chen took my mother's demureness as bitchy obstinacy, another rejection. But my mother didn't want to tell Chen how sick she was feeling; as if to bring it into words was to permit it, and to permit it was to strengthen it. A virulent nausea was by then eating into her, so discombobulating she felt both too heavy and too light at the same time. Her period had disappeared. She was drinking water by the gallon, but her skin was strangely parched and her nails had become dry with ridges.

My mother left Chen at the pool. She needed to wash her hair; it would take the best part of the afternoon, the washing, the oiling, the ironing, the arranging. Padding back to her room, she steeled herself for the event. Her hair had been coming out, every day, more. When she brushed it at night, the brush's bristles would become entirely knit over with strays after only a few strokes. Through fear of what might happen, she hadn't washed her hair in two weeks, putting in her suitcase the hotel shampoo bottles that maids across America liked to leave every day like a reminder. Now rinsing out the shampoo in the bath, strands of hair were swimming around her, sticking to her skin. My mother carefully collected her hair in the bath, gliding her hand through the water. When she unplugged the drain, she made sure not to let any strands go down.

She sat on the edge of the big Miami hotel bed and began picking apart the mass, counting. If there were more than two or three hundred at the most, she told herself, she'd know something was wrong. Every few strands she'd find a hair that felt different than the others, like an old woman's hair, crinkly and desiccated, as if its moisture was being sapped from the root. When she reached four hundred hairs, there was a knock at the door and without waiting for an answer Ronen Chen came right in with his stage directions for her extra solo. He saw my mother, sitting in a sagging towel with spiders of wet hair all over her hands and a plastic hotel wastepaper basket between her legs, crying. Wordlessly, he left my mother's room, folding up her solo.

ONCE WHEN I was a child, having my hair endlessly brushed by my mother, I asked her why she kept her own hair so short, in a haircut like a bowl, when she would not let me get a haircut at all. "When there is a baby in a mommy's tummy, mommy has for hair no energy," said my mother. I asked my mother why she didn't grow her hair back, now that I was a big kid. My mother shook her head no, as if in a family unit there was only so much energy to go around. She reminded me how much I liked it when she did my hair in hundreds of tiny braids, with beads and orthodontist elastics, like Bo Derek on the beach. "If I want to brush hair," she said, "I can always brush your hair."

AS THE *SHALOM ISRAEL!* night approached, the emotional pitch of the house began changing. Some timely hormone was filling in spaces, the smell of something beginning or ending. It didn't matter that my mother had not been in contact with Ronen Chen for several decades, she'd convinced herself of something, and now she was in the throes of a self-generating checklist of minute personal preparations, so hyper she couldn't even sit to watch TV. She said the dance competition shows had become boring and she didn't like hearing about the war in Gaza during the newsbreaks, but the truth was her heart was pounding through her chest.

With the TV den free of my mother, I spent my days lying there on the sofa, trying to stay out of the airstream of her spinning wheels. Sometimes, when I emerged from the room, I'd find things in the house changed, small things, an umbrella stand taken out of the vestibule and put into the front closet, plants moved from hall to landing, pictures rearranged. While I'd been in hospital, I'd made a small collection of op-art needlepoint pillows, sending my husband out for more intricate patterns with every failed surgery and botched procedure. My mother had now taken them off the living room sofa and put them into the linen cupboard. I then caught her throwing out a tea cozy that I actually used almost daily and she said she had to because the tea cozy was both ugly and weird. I recognized my mother's impulse as a kind usually having to do with shame: the sudden need to empty a closet of various evocations, to not live one moment longer with a certain bedspread, to repaint a kitchen for reasons nobody else can understand. She'd rolled up the enormous midnight blue flat-weave rug in the guest bedroom, lifting up the queen bed herself to do it.

"I don't like this dark blue carpet in my bedroom," she'd said, pointing to my exquisite Italian rug, now reduced to a flaccid cylinder leaning on the upstairs banister. "Don't you feel like the floor is hard on your heels?" I asked, feeling something like outrage. "No. I have very strong feet," she said. "I'm not like you with the slippers."

THE EVENING OF *Shalom Israel!*, I sat on the guest room bed in my housecoat while my mother sat at the vanity, getting ready. I flipped through her novel by the Israeli writer about the child lost to war and saw that my mother was on the same page she'd been on a week before. I imagined my mother lying where I was, trying to read, the same paragraph looping like a scratched record, and getting up exasperated and ready to wreak a bit more havoc on my decor. I looked at the bare floor and felt my heart bleed a little, thinking how no comfortable state could lead a woman to pull up the carpet in a house that isn't even her own.

I had told my mother earlier in the day that I didn't feel well enough to go to Place des Arts that evening. I knew she had a plan in mind for the night, and it did not really involve a slow-moving daughter inching her way out of some vapourish ghetto of illness. It involved more swanning into places to joyous shrieks of delight. If I had been my mother, I would have imagined the same thing for myself, the dramatic reunion. Ronen Chen would see how fit and lovely and preserved by the Canadian cold my mother was and over cocktails at the hotel later that night he'd invite her to join the tour, and they'd pick up where they left off so many years prior.

My mother turned from the vanity and reached for a black glossy shopping bag on the bed. Over the week, she'd been shopping. "Look," she said, removing a wide leather belt, studded with gold and patched with ovals of faux zebra fur. "This belt you wear on your hips," she said, lowering her knees to get a good view in the vanity mirror. She laid the belt on the bed, near a new cowl-neck sweater dress, and new nylon pantyhose still in the package. The photo from Miami was set atop her purse. She'd already told me that the picture was her ticket backstage.

"Did you phone anyone to make arrangements to get to the performers?" I now asked, watching my mother lick a cotton swab and grind it into a small pot of crumbly kohl.

"For what *arrangements*?" she asked, expertly stroking the swab over her eyelid. "I know Place des Arts. Very good I know it."

"Mom, there's going to be crazy security. How are you going to get backstage?"

"Don't make in your head problems," she said. "Somebody will see me. I have the picture."

MY MOTHER LEFT the house wearing my most glamorous coat, full-length mohair with a braided gold-tasselled belt and a fox collar, a coat for high heels and deep impressions. I hadn't worn it in six years. It would be big of me to give the coat to my mother, I thought, kissing her goodbye, already anticipating how the house would be lighter after *Shalom Israel!*; the static of anticipation tamped down.

I went back up to my mother's room to make sure none of her dirty Q-tips or crumbling kohl had landed on the carpet, and felt paradoxically relieved when I arrived upstairs to remember that the rug had been rolled up. My heart was tired, my legs weak for some familiar reasons and some reasons I could truly barely fathom, something having to do with mothers and daughters, about who gets to pull more at any time.

I made up her messy bed, and folded all the clothes on
the floor and put her books and papers in neat piles by
her bedside. I lay on the bed for a minute to rest, careful
not to wrinkle its smoothed spread.

I wanted my mother to come home to a nice room.
Among her papers, I had found pamphlets for condo
properties in Tel Aviv, my mother once again giving
new life to an old challenge. She had threatened to
move back to Israel so many times when I was young
that even now I imagined that if she went, I would go
too. I still carry with me a scene, another from that
heartbreaking summer in Tel Aviv, sitting with my
mother at my aunt's house in a sweltering heat wave.
Across a plate of watermelon sat a fat, horrible woman,
a real estate agent with visible drips mingling with
stretch marks down her cleavage. She was showing
my mother pictures of high-security tower apartments,
apartments she said were good for a woman with no
husband. Between these depressing properties, the fat
woman kept on remarking how my mother's Hebrew
was so quaintly sixties, how listening to her was like
a time warp, and how it was so wonderful that my
mother knew all the old milk-and-honey songs and
dances, those old patriotic cultural concoctions that
had nothing to do with the country anymore.

I RETURNED TO the TV den, and turned on the evening news. There were demonstrations outside Place des Arts, a burning flag, hundreds of placards: ISRAËL CRIMINEL DE GUERRE! PALESTINE LIBRE! ISRAËL TERRORISTE! I imagined the packed concert hall, not a seat to spare, the plainclothes security mingled in with the audience. I imagined the bag-checking guards sealing every door, the picture of my mother and the choreographer of her career meaningless to them as they rifled through her purse looking for lipstick grenades. I imagined my mother in her nosebleed X seat in the hot, heavy mohair coat, trapped in an airtight atmosphere of expertly forced Israeli elation.

THE FOLLOWING MORNING, she wasn't up before me. I made a nice breakfast for us, French toast and maple syrup, coffee and juice, fabric napkins, and saucers under the cups. I listened to the radio while preparing it. There was an interview that I didn't want to miss, one with that Israeli author my mother had been reading, the one who had lost his son in the last Lebanon war while writing a novel about a parent losing their child to war. Even though the author was in North America doing readings and giving interviews, it felt almost cosmically coincidental that his voice would be in my kitchen that Sunday, as if the preoccupations of my house and that of the world outside were finally on the same page. I got my mother out of bed, and gave her coffee quietly so that we could listen together.

"You know his son was killed in Lebanon, in the last war," she said, loudly scraping excess syrup off her toast during an interlude between the author's words. "You missed that war, you were too sick. It was a stupid war—"

"Well, I—"

"Shhh!" said my mother as the author began speaking again. He talked about the strangeness of having a bestseller and a dead son. My mother held her toast unchewed in her mouth to better hear. His Hebrew sounded exactly like hers.

"He doesn't understand why his life became the way it is," said my mother, swallowing during a pause in the author's words. "I can hear in his voice—he doesn't understand what happened at all." Satisfied with what she knew about the author, having made her decision about the state of him, my mother began leafing through the paper. There was no review of *Shalom Israel!*, just coverage of the demonstrations outside it. I understood that my mother never got backstage. She watched the show, just an audience member, and then came home.

"You don't feel like you need to get out of the house?" she asked me, still peering deeply into the Weekend section. She said there was a place that was having 75 percent off Persian rugs; there was a new pedestrian path along the Lachine Canal; there were three open houses in the neighbourhood. She licked the tip of a pencil and began circling things in the paper, some new plan forming.

"You should go and get dressed," she said, gathering our breakfast dishes. "I'll wash these." I went upstairs. I ran the bath. My mother then yelled up and told me to stop running the bath because I was making the kitchen-sink water run cold. I turned the faucet off and sat on the tub and waited for her to finish.

COMPLIMENTARITY

MARIE-LAURE ARRIVED AT ELSA'S house in a flurry of long scarves and auburn hair dusted with snow. Elsa and Marie-Laure had not been such dear friends when Marie-Laure still lived in Montreal, but since Maman had died, and the divorce from Roger, and since Marie-Laure had moved to Nantes to write her new book, there had been so many letters, such closeness, and soon Marie-Laure announced that she could no longer stand it anymore, she *had* to fly back from France and see her dear, dear Elsa. Could Elsa bear such a visitor? Was there just the smallest, tiniest guest room chez *la belle Elsa*?

Elsa was flattered to have so many bright words sprinkled in her direction. She hadn't been feeling normal. Of course she hadn't: the loss of a mother remains the loss of a mother, even for a woman of sixty-five; and then the divorce, humiliatingly, after forty years of marriage; and now this thin, mean simplicity—everything, always, alone.

Lately, Elsa asked the maid to draw the curtains earlier in the day and went to bed soon after the maid left in the evening. She'd calculated that it was better to be buttering toast with the radio at 5 a.m. than up with the television turning her bedroom a ghostly blue at night.

Most days she sat in her new home office. Elsa had been a patron of the Montreal Museum of Fine Arts Ball for decades, but this year she volunteered to do more than just sit on the board. She was head of Raffles, Gifts, and Door Prizes. It was not a job for which an office was entirely necessary, but she'd needed to do something with Roger's old dressing room, and so she'd made a project of it. There were now shelves and filing drawers where his jackets and trousers once hung. The walls were papered with a shell-coloured damask, and a large Directoire desk that had once centred Maman's library was now Elsa's computer table.

Elsa liked sitting in the room, a very small room, more than anywhere else in the house. Since Roger left, she was too often seized by a peculiar feeling of windy exposure. Sometimes it was as if the floorboards had been removed from under her feet. When she made her phone calls for the ball, asking for donations, she could hear her voice waver with anxiety when the person at the other end began singsonging conclusions, about to hang up, everyone so busy, their time so crowded, making the overquiet of the house shrill in Elsa's ears, a silence like judgement.

So the idea of Marie-Laure's visit brought a small, pleasing flutter to Elsa's chest, a medallion of dignity. A *friend*. A person electing to come and visit. And when Marie-Laure arrived, with three pieces of luggage, and walked through Elsa's ground floor, snow dripping from her hair, hand fluttering with astonishment as she surveyed the newly decorated rooms, Elsa felt almost dumbstruck with happiness.

"*Ma chère, ma chère*," said Marie-Laure. "I am *en amour fou*. It is the house of *une dame de grand caractère*! I can see the great parties you will have here. Oh, I can see so much."

Last year, when all of Maman's containers began arriving from Paris, and Elsa had begun the integration of their contents into the house, Roger had said that he didn't like living in a museum.

"I know it's all priceless," he said, unkindly swiping his hand over the top of a bronze mirror, a rococo, still shrouded in thick plastic wrapping, and just that day hatched from its crate. "And I know your mother's death was difficult, but —"

Elsa busied her hands to block her ears, tearing at the mirror's tape and plastic. She'd heard it before. *I need Space. I need Breathing Room.* Roger had said that Elsa had become madly material, that with the arrival of Maman's things, all this *décor*, she'd become obsessed. He didn't understand. There comes a time when you must collect your history. You must collect it where you can find it, or it risks fading to nothingness.

But Elsa didn't say this to Roger. To Roger, she could only cry that she'd grown up with these things. She didn't want to get rid of them now — *couldn't*. She'd once heard someone on the radio, an author, say that single people in the country were less lonely than singles in the city because they were surrounded by trees and animals. Elsa was of course a city person, and not at that time single, but she understood the concept: a tethering fullness. The requirement of bumpers, borders, sops against pain. Animals or upholstery, it was a question of absorption of reverberation, of echo.

"And by the way, that mirror *could* hang in a museum," said Elsa. Roger's jowls were shaking with annoyance. Lately he was angry with anything she did. Elsa was the one who had lost her mother, and yet it was his moods that required tiptoeing around. She had to veer into things: *I am making myself salad and cold roast beef for lunch. If you want, I could make some extra.*

"I had to fight to get this mirror here," continued Elsa. "The Ministère de la Culture said it should be in the Louvre! They said 'what good will it do anyone in Canada?'"

"And your answer?" yelled Roger. "'I need to make my house as stifling as my mother's was'? And now nobody around here can walk two paces before shinning themselves on some planter or fucking footstool?"

It was as if for every piece Elsa installed, Roger became more remote. It was as if he had created some personal see-saw that could only stack against Elsa, catapulting Roger out of the house, making it seem like it was Elsa's fault, all that heaviness on her side.

Roger said that if Elsa didn't watch it, she'd simply *become* her mother. "Alone in too many rooms full of too much stuff. It can't end well, Elsa."

Earlier that week, she had come into Roger's dressing room to find that he had removed the Victorian cherry wood clothes horse, a piece from Maman's that Elsa thought he'd find useful. He'd also taken down the Redouté prints of birds' nests that hadn't even been Maman's but had always hung in the room. He had replaced them with a single Asian-looking calligraphy which was just an inky circle. Roger lowered his voice reverentially when explaining the print to Elsa. He said it was drawn by a famous Vietnamese monk. He said it represented emptiness.

"Of what?" asked Elsa, wanting to seem open-minded.

"Of everything," answered her husband.

"But why is that good?" asked Elsa.

WALKING UP TO the guest room, Elsa stopped to show Marie-Laure her new home office.

"It smells wonderful in here, *ma chère*," said Marie-Laure, breathing in deeply.

The room had proved difficult to divest of the sourdough smell of Roger's clothes and shoes. Elsa told her friend how she'd made a regime of burning scented candles, how she happened to have a surplus of scented candles, donations for the ball that were going unused.

"I thought we should include the candles in the gift bags," said Elsa, opening the room's walk-in closet. "But some of the women on the board said they smelled like 'old lady.'"

Marie-Laure stepped into the closet, gasping in a small, dramatic way.

"*Ma chère*, what is this closet of wonders?"

The stockpile was vast: not just stacks of expensive candles, but what looked like hundreds of pairs of Chanel sunglasses, several full-length bags from Fourrures Fendi, a skyline of boxes from Cristofle, and a large plastic bin with an Yves St. Laurent sticker pasted on top, filled with silver key chains.

"These are the prizes and gifts for the ball," said Elsa. "People have been so generous. *Too* generous —" She bent down to reach a low shelf and removed a box filled with certificates.

"Look at these," she said, pulling out one of the cards, a voucher for three hundred dollars at La Clinique Nesselrode. Nesselrode's was where you went to get your face fixed; the place said to have the most embarrassing waiting room in all of Montreal. "They arrived unsolicited. The board said it would be impossible to give these out."

"Oh yes," said Marie-Laure, rounding her eyes. "Some things must remain one's *petit secret.*"

Marie-Laure had been to the ball the year before. She'd caused a sensation, arriving on the arm of the newly widowed billionaire Benno Goldschlag, who was in his eighties. The women on the board saw it in the worst possible way—a little gold digger. Benno's wife, Helgi, was barely cold—but Elsa thought they were just jealous. Marie-Laure was single, and beautiful, and a published writer. A career woman. Elsa said she had seen her name once in a Québécois fashion magazine. She'd written an article about creativity. "Finding your Feminine Creativity," it was called.

"Creativity my foot," said one of the board members. "Creative in getting old rich men's telephone numbers."

But the gossip soon abated because Marie-Laure left for Nantes within weeks of her appearance with Goldschlag.

"Do you ever speak to Benno Goldschlag?" asked Elsa, bringing Marie-Laure up another flight to the guest room, where she'd put a jug of fresh water, a vase with a few white roses, some books she thought her friend might be interested in.

"Oh, *ma chère*, he was just, I don't know, *random*," said Marie-Laure, falling back on the bed. "Wow! I feel like I am in a hotel. Oh! And I have a little *prezzie. Pour toi!*"

Elsa watched Marie-Laure dig around a large red handbag, a soft thing, with drooping tassels. How was it possible that Marie-Laure was only ten years her junior? She seemed so much younger. Elsa wore a camel dress and matching cardigan, and the gulf between these pieces and Marie-Laure's form-fitting, V-necked sweater, narrow jeans, and studded flats seemed like it could contain several generations of women, a span so vast it abated any possibility of envy. Marie-Laure's legs were long pliant tubes, with an airy space between the thighs that Elsa hadn't seen on herself since her twenties. Her cheeks had a taut, upsweeping aerodynamicism. Women used to say "good bones," but even this descriptor felt outdated for Marie-Laure, who seemed to Elsa a woman sculpted and buffed by activity.

"*Ah! Voilà!*" said Marie-Laure, producing from her

bag, unwrapped, as if it had just fallen in, a thick black bangle with a diamanté starburst at its centre.

"It's so original!" said Elsa. "Oh! It's heavy!"

"It's ebony," said Marie-Laure. "I found it in Nantes. It spoke to me. It said, 'Please grab me from the shelf, *ma chère!*' It can go daytime or evening. Of course, it is not real diamonds. *Une demi-vérité.*"

In letters, Elsa had written to Marie-Laure how there was too little taking her out of the house, either daytime or evening. Once in a while, she would walk to the bakery down the street to have lunch, and then lose her nerve. Nearing the place, she would see herself as others might: a woman the age of a grandmother, alone with a bowl of soup and a humiliating pastry. She would end up taking her food home, in a bag. She'd have it at the kitchen table, feeling silly, because her fridge was full of better things.

BEFORE MARIE-LAURE'S ARRIVAL. Elsa had spent the day preparing their dinner. She made the foods she most enjoyed cooking, which also happened to be the ones Roger had last year stopped being able to stomach. Elsa would make his favourite meals—she recalled in particular a *boeuf en croûte*—and he would respond with the strangest excuses for why he could no longer tolerate the foods he once relished.

"I'm on a detox," he'd say. "I've cut out gluten." He would eat, grubbing in silence, at the kitchen table from plastic bags of nuts and seeds and "ancient grains" for which he'd made a corner between the biscuits and the jams in the pantry. He seemed increasingly to subsist on what he once would have named birdseed, hamster food, never mind the mouldy connotations of ancient grains.

For Marie-Laure, Elsa hoped she had not gone overboard with creamy watercress soup and braised lamb and baked dauphinoise potatoes. While she chopped and mixed and grated, she thought of the good discussions she'd have with her friend over dinner. But now that Marie-Laure was actually at the table, Elsa found her brain cramped like a fist clenched for too long. Decent sentences simply would not squeeze out. Over the soup, Marie-Laure asked about the divorce, and even this juicy topic turned stale on Elsa's tongue. She could only repeat that she was fine, just fine. You know, things happen, such is life.

"But you are obviously coping so well," said Marie-Laure, pushing her bowl towards the centre of the table, still half full.

Elsa considered sharing the circumstances of Maman's death, which required no great art for dramatic telling, but then decided the risk of it darkening this first evening was too high.

Instead, she took the soup bowls into the kitchen. When she returned to the dining room with two plates heavy with lamb, Marie-Laure was examining herself in the gilded rococo mirror hanging on the room's far wall.

"Oh, I do look awful in this old mirror," said Marie-Laure, gathering her hair into a ponytail, while pulling her temples with the flats of her palms. "Strange how you get used to seeing yourself in the same mirrors, and then when you see yourself in a different one, *c'est plus la même histoire*—"

Elsa stood with the two plates in her hands. "Why don't we sit now," she said. "For the mains."

Marie-Laure turned her head to Elsa and gave a glamorous smile, a smile of indulgences and special confidences. "I have so much to tell you about my book," she said, squeezing her shoulders inwards and tippytoeing to her chair. "I hope you have a very large patience. Yes?"

Elsa nodded, and before she'd even had a chance to sit down, Marie-Laure was dashing out of the room to get her laptop. Elsa watched the backs of Marie-Laure's legs, which met in wishbone formation, at a seam wedging between two jeans pockets. Marie-Laure's shape was not just sexy, thought Elsa, but that of someone who still really had it. Had sex. One could imagine Marie-Laure naked. And lovely. Elsa, herself, could not fathom standing naked in front of anybody now. Her intimate life with Roger had for many years been no life at all, worn away by decades of familiarity, and by the creeping indignities of age. It got to the point where it had just become simpler to ignore the odd impulse, and then to be thankful as the impulses abated altogether.

She wondered now if this qualified her as frigid. There did not used to be such a thing as frigid at sixty-five; just sexless, which was normal. But Elsa knew rules were changing. One woman on the museum ball board—seventy if a day—was known this year to have had a reconstruction, for looseness, *vaginal*. And it wasn't so much that she was having the surgery that caught Elsa by surprise as much as that she was sufficiently active to require it. It made Elsa ask if Roger— who she was now sure *had* been having sex before he left—also had a decent reason for the divorce. Maybe Elsa had not been providing enough in that department.

Marie-Laure returned with her white laptop already open and humming.

"This is for my book," she said, putting the machine on the polished table.

"Is the book finished, then?" asked Elsa.

"This is an important part of the project," replied Marie-Laure.

"But is it published?"

"Oh, I will only consider publishing it myself," said Marie-Laure, sniffily, turning her laptop in Elsa's direction. "With investors. I will be having a few meetings about this while I am here."

"So you are looking for patronage?" asked Elsa.

"*Oof!* That sounds too stuffy," said Marie-Laure.

Elsa told her friend she knew one man who'd published his own book, a retired corporate lawyer. It was called *When in Doubt—Sue!* It was a humour book.

"*Chérie*, shhh!" said Marie-Laure, pointing at the screen with her chin. It read:

ENTER THE UNIVERSE BEYOND "SELF-HELP"

Words began zooming into the foreground, soon joined by a changing roster of photos of Marie-Laure posing on a beach in a flowing white dress with a piece of voile, then in a business suit with a briefcase, then in an open shirt with the collar turned up:

Integrity

Kinship

Rigour

Unique Dreams

Optimizing Creativity

Complimentarity

"What is complimentarity?" asked Elsa, picking up her fork.

"It's part of my systems theory," said Marie-Laure.

"What is systems theory?"

Elsa's meat was a little overdone. Marie-Laure had still not touched hers. Her bony wrist was bent over the mouse pad, the veins of her hand bulging, making it look older than the body from which it came.

"It's a theory about the nature of all things—" said Marie-Laure, distractedly. "Shit!—you're supposed to be able to click on these pictures—"

Elsa thought of Roger's Vietnamese circle. Empty of everything.

"Is systems theory like Buddhism?" asked Elsa.

"It's better than Buddhism," said Marie-Laure. "People live in fear of proactive creativity, of awakening their inner modalities—"

While Marie-Laure talked, Elsa nodded as if she was thinking very hard. The way Marie-Laure was speaking—sentences made of words that did not seem to match—made Elsa question if old words had taken on new meanings.

"Is what we are looking at your web site?" interrupted Elsa. Elsa wanted very much to pose certain questions having to do with web sites.

"This? It's still under construction," answered Marie-Laure, now sliding her plate off the placemat, to make better room for her computer.

"Is this what you would call an online CV, then?"

asked Elsa. An online CV had been the thing Roger had originally needed. A location for his research projects. He had hired a web site designer, the daughter of an old colleague, not quite a favour, he said, but close. She was twenty-eight, with wild curly blond hair that looked peculiarly dry and attractive at the same time. The designer would sometimes hitch her hair up with one of the many bands she wore around her wrist. The web site designer's hair made Elsa look at her own carefully curled-under bob one evening and muss it up, just to see what it would do. She looked like a hysteric.

"An online CV?" asked Marie-Laure, irritated.

"Yes," said Elsa, ashamed of her question. It was clearly the wrong question. But she had many others that she felt Marie-Laure could help with. They were all categorized together in her mind. They included: How long did it usually take to design a web site? And was it normal for young women who created web sites to wear tight yoga clothes when working with clients? And what was the stylistic meaning of those elastics? Or of wearing two thin headbands at the front of the head and a high trailing ponytail at the back? Was it a kind of Athenian look? Did it have anything to do with ancient grains or with monks who drew empty circles?

THE NEXT DAY. Elsa made breakfast for two. She used silver for the tea, and Maman's gold-rimmed porcelain for the croissants, but Marie-Laure slept in, and then was so busy with book meetings that Elsa didn't see her until the evening, when Marie-Laure left for dinner with a "very important potential investor."

Elsa hadn't imagined that Marie-Laure's meetings would be quite so numerous. She'd imagined more time together. She'd looked up films and concerts for the week. She'd even fantasized about going shopping with Marie-Laure and buying something extravagant for her friend; something Marie-Laure would never be able to buy herself. But now Elsa was increasingly seized by an unhappy desire to take Marie-Laure by the shoulders and say, *Please just stop moving.* Marie-Laure's methods in sourcing investment seemed too eccentric. She had gone to her daytime meetings in the tubelike jeans, and to her business dinner in a slinky, open-backed dress.

The following morning, Elsa made a more elaborate spread for breakfast. There was now croissants and toast and fresh strawberries and compote and coffee and thick Greek yogurt spooned into two gold-rimmed ramekins, then swiped flat with the side of a knife. Elsa had garnished each ramekin with a piece of sliced berry in the centre, like a miniature heart. Marie-Laure would need nerve to meet this breakfast with the same busy wind behind her back.

"YOU MAKE ME feel like a fool," Elsa had told Roger.

This was towards the end. She'd offered him a plate of cold roast beef and salad for lunch and he'd looked at her like she was mad.

"I didn't ask for lunch," he said. "I don't want lunch. It's like the less I want, the more you give. It's almost as if you have a tic."

WHEN MARIE-LAURE DIDN'T come down by ten, Elsa took the coffee she was drinking upstairs to her home office. *I can be busy too,* she thought. *It's not as if I don't have work.*

While the beige computer warmed up, Elsa opened the drawer of Maman's Directoire desk. She was fishing for a coaster when Marie-Laure came into the room unannounced, and in her coat. She inhaled sharply when she saw Elsa.

"*Ma chère*! I thought you were in the kitchen," she said, hand to her chest. "Having your beautiful breakfast. I just—I need some envelopes."

Elsa went into the closet for envelopes while Marie-Laure resumed talking, her words gaining speed as if she wanted no air between them.

"Woo, those stairs, *ma belle*. No wonder you keep such a good figure. Phew! Well. Wonderful. So much space. And this office. So perfect. For your *affaires d'état*. Ha, ha—"

"Well, just setting up for a bit of work..." said Elsa, trailing off. "The raffles, gifts..."

Marie-Laure nodded without interest, gazing in the direction of the closet. Elsa gave Marie-Laure the envelopes. Marie-Laure barely glanced at them.

"Aren't those what you wanted?" asked Elsa. "I have big yellow ones, too—"

Marie-Laure snapped to attention. "Yes! Wonderful. Forgive me. I am simply—" and here Marie-Laure waved her hands at either side of her head and fluttered her eyelids. "Crazy, crazy."

Elsa had decided not to be insulted that Marie-Laure hadn't asked about Maman's death yet. Marie-Laure, Elsa had noticed, never spoke of her own family, either. There was a type, thought Elsa: somehow self-formed; wary of connections; immune to loneliness. You could barely imagine them with parents, siblings, children. Maman may have been of that sort herself.

"Who are you meeting with today?" asked Elsa, squeezing stiff words from a tightening chest. It was childish, the way Marie-Laure made Elsa feel intrusive whenever Elsa asked anything about these meetings.

"An investor," said Marie-Laure.

"Who?" said Elsa.

"The CEO of Argento-Québec," mumbled Marie-Laure.

"Oh! Jean-Marie Gélinas?" asked Elsa. She knew

Jean-Marie: a cold, elegant French Canadian, never out of a suit and tie, who would cut you short midsentence if he knew where your words were going. Elsa was surprised he'd given Marie-Laure a meeting. Just that year, he'd turned down chairing the museum ball, finally sending a cheque to the fundraising committee with the words *"Now please stop phoning"* scrawled on a business card attached. She couldn't imagine him sitting through five minutes of Marie-Laure's *complimentarity*.

Marie-Laure looked aggravated by Elsa's familiarity with Jean-Marie Gélinas. "He's very interested, it just so happens," she said, adjusting her coat's belt.

Elsa had noticed before that the coat—a creamy, brushed cashmere with a broad lapel and a brandy-coloured lining—was of a richer cloth than most of Marie-Laure's other clothes. It wasn't that the other clothes were in bad taste. Not really. Just that this coat was unusually tasteful.

"Bon," said Marie-Laure, "my taxi must be outside."

AFTER HER FRIEND left, Elsa returned to the kitchen. She looked down at the uneaten breakfast spread; at the ramekins of yogurt, so carefully prepared. There was no reason to feel any shame in these two gold-rimmed things sitting there separately, each with its precise berry garnish bleeding pink like a tiny mockery at the centre. Elsa rinsed them out herself while looking out the kitchen window. She saw the back of Marie-Laure's cream coat quite a way down the street. The winter's snow was melting, making little rivers run down along the sidewalks. Perhaps the taxi hadn't come, she thought, now watching the white yogurt slip down the drain with the water. Perhaps there hadn't been a taxi to begin with.

It was good to have the yogurt down the drain.

Maman's suicide:

Sixteen sleeping pills
Two cups of yogurt
The yogurt taken so that the pills didn't come up.

Maman had a highlighted cheat sheet provided by a euthanasia society in France, a Xeroxed page from a book titled *Liberté Finale*. The book said nothing about putting the pills in a small silver dish and the yogurt in eighteenth-century Delftware, but Maman had. She was found in full makeup and wearing a good suit: pink tweed with black braid. In the jacket's gold-buttoned pocket was a note, directing Elsa to a large manila envelope in the Directoire desk in the library.

There were nearly one hundred pages of instructions—the movers, the packers, the auction houses, the insurance, the government agencies, the estate agent, plus a complete list of all the objects of worth in the house. It must have taken Maman months to write. When Elsa telephoned the estate agent who would sell the family apartment in Paris, he said, "Yes, I just last week received a letter from your mother. She said you would be phoning right about now."

WHEN MARIE-LAURE RETURNED that evening, she was wearing sunglasses. Elsa greeted her friend in the front hall, but Marie-Laure simply shook her head silently, making her way to the stairs.

"Marie-Laure," said Elsa. "Have you been crying?" Upon closer inspection, it actually looked worse than that. There was yellow—the beginnings of bruising—at the crest of Marie-Laure's upper lip, which was badly swollen, and around the folds of her nose. A cheekbone was puffy, too. It looked like she'd been punched in the face.

"Oh, it's nothing," said Marie-Laure, hitching her red bag onto her shoulder. "Just a hard day."

"Marie-Laure, did something happen?" said Elsa, watching her friend disappear up the staircase. "Did something happen with Jean-Marie Gélinas?"

"I will say good night now," said Marie-Laure, yelling down. "No dinner for me. I am too tired." And then Elsa heard the door to the guest room slam shut.

Alone at the kitchen table, again, Elsa had scrambled eggs with lots of butter. She knew something was going on but found she had almost no stomach to imagine what. She'd done too much of that sort of thinking with Roger before he left: *maybe he's sick, maybe there's been an accident, maybe something terrible that has nothing to do with me.*

Elsa wished it didn't bother her that Marie-Laure was going dinnerless because she was ashamed of something—ashamed of something Elsa didn't even *want* to know about!—but it did bother her. She got up to make two more eggs.

The last time Elsa climbed to this room with a tray, it had been to bring some sandwiches to Roger and the web designer. They'd been up there for hours. She hadn't meant to intrude. She knew that Roger liked being with the designer, alone on the second floor. His mood would grow expansive before the girl's arrival. Elsa had thought his affection only natural, harmless, healthy, even. She was a beautiful girl. But when Elsa reached the room, not knocking because of the tray, and smiling behind her offering, Roger chastised her so sharply—"We don't *want* anything. We can survive an hour without *needing* anything"—that Elsa was trembling when she put the sandwiches down.

Elsa could still call up the backs of their heads, the rinds of her husband's big ears, the girl's pretty nape, framed by the blue of the computer screen they were both staring into. She hadn't walked in on anything.

But when the girl left that evening, she'd looked at Elsa with soft eyes while collecting her jacket and mouthed, "I'm sorry," silently, with her lips only. Elsa did not understand everything yet, but it was then that she'd sensed a shift, a limbic feeling, the weight of some still-nameless news. A girl of twenty-eight was apologizing for her husband's behaviour.

Elsa now made her footfalls approaching the bedroom loud, to alert Marie-Laure that she was coming, but also to stake her claim on the action: *This is my house. You are my guest.*

There was no answer when she knocked. Managing the tray with a raised knee, Elsa turned the knob. The door opened to reveal Marie-Laure sitting up in bed, her bruised face now spackled with some shiny salve. She was watching a movie on her laptop with headphones on, eating a muffin with a canned soft drink. A plastic DVD case was open on the bed, surrounded by the plastic it had come wrapped in. Near it was a paper bag from the bakery down the hill. Elsa noticed the packaging—and how it pointed to a planned sequestering—as one might receive a knife through the sternum.

Marie-Laure removed the headphones and put her unfinished muffin in the paper bag, her swollen lips pursed, her movements becoming quicker the longer Elsa stood there with the tray. Elsa could hear the tinny tinkle of music and banter through the headphones on the bed.

"I thought you were crying—" said Elsa, the tray rattling a bit. "Or maybe, Jean-Marie—I don't know. I wondered if he'd *hurt* you —"

Marie-Laure put her greased forehead in her hand and sighed loudly. Her auburn hair fell before her like a curtain. She didn't speak for a long time. Elsa could not get a good look at her face.

"I just need some privacy," she finally said, as if to herself, massaging her brow. "You are always following me around with food — it's really too bizarre!"

BETRAYAL HAS A point of conversion, a crux where the victim careens to clarity. That evening, Elsa went to sleep still a dupe. The following morning, she woke up knowing it.

It made all the difference. She waited in bed until she heard Marie-Laure leave the house, and then she went up to the guest bedroom. Marie-Laure's clothes were everywhere. A pair of jeans was hung inside out off a chair back, a damp bathrobe was left on the bed, a sweater was slung over a hanger slat messily, its label cut out. Elsa remembered Maman doing that when she bought cheap birthday gifts for maids. Take the label out. Tell them you bought it on avenue Montaigne.

She looked in Marie-Laure's luggage first, then in her handbags (the giant red tasselled one was not even leather), then, finally, her pockets. When she'd summoned the nerve to do this to Roger's jackets, she'd found her evidence very quickly, a receipt for a dinner obviously for two, two mains and two drinks and two teas and two desserts at a café called Vegan D-Lite.

He said it was a "meeting." For his web site.

"Nobody eats something called Flourless Goddess Brownies at a legitimate meeting!" screamed Elsa, reading off the bill. "And *Eggless Omelet*! I don't even know what that is!" It was like even the food was involved in her shaming. Just the night prior, Elsa had been so embarrassed by the sight of another meal—gigot d'agneau, fully dressed—left untouched by her husband—"I've quit red meat," he said—that she'd pushed the whole thing, bone and all, down the sink's garbage disposal.

"It's tofu," said Roger, unnervingly calm.

"What?"

"The eggless omelet. It's tofu."

"But you don't even like tofu!" cried Elsa.

Roger had grown so thin. The bones below his eyes protruded hungrily, stretching the skin strangely across his nose. He had more lines, some now even slashing down his cheeks, but also a certain angular lankiness that echoed the look of youth, if not quite achieving it.

"I do like tofu," said Roger. "I like it *a lot*."

The day after Elsa had found the Vegan D-Lite receipt, she'd found an even fuller narrative in a blazer pocket—a Vedic Bliss Retreat bill where a plasticized convention name tag would usually be. Roger finally gave his admission. He said he'd been "seeing Amy" for a year. Elsa counted the last twelve months in milestones. Maman's death, then packing the apartment in Paris, then the shipments arriving in Montreal. Roger made it seem as if Elsa's ignorance of his affair made her the more delinquent between them. Everyone else in Montreal knew.

Elsa found all she needed in a single pocket of Marie-Laure's cream coat—or rather a single pocket of Helgi Goldschlag's cream coat—Helgi, the late wife of the billionaire Benno. Would Benno have given this little parvenu his wife's fine old coat? Unlikely. But here was Helgi's name embroidered in the satin lining. While rifling, Elsa had also found a tangle of Yves Saint Laurent key chains and three pairs of Chanel sunglasses. She thought of Marie-Laure's veined, ugly hands cradling her puffy, lineless face the night prior. She knew what she was looking for before she'd found it: a thick pad of folded receipts from La Clinique Nesselrode, and everything—Botox, fillers, lasers—paid for by gift certificate.

After that, things moved quickly. Elsa called the maid up and gave her instructions to wash and fold and press all of Marie-Laure's things perfectly. "And then pack them in her suitcase," said Elsa. "As if packing for a duchess." Back in her garret in Nantes, Marie-Laure would open her luggage, and understand what Elsa knew, the Goldschlag coat folded inside out and placed monogram side up at the top of the suitcase, along with the black starburst bangle that Marie-Laure had given to Elsa. A common thief.

When Marie-Laure ran up the stairs asking why her suitcase was in the front hall, Elsa said, "Why not ask Dr. Nesselrode? Maybe he will give you the answer."

It was not what one would have called "a zinger." But Elsa did not let herself think up better retorts when going over these moments on the phone. *She said she was going to meetings, but really she was just getting face injections! With the ball's gift certificates! Stolen! And she stole key chains! And a coat! Poor dead Helgi's coat!* The telephone crackled with laughter in Elsa's home office. She now kept the window inched open. Tiny spring buds blew onto the Directoire desk, a piece that now belonged to Elsa alone.

FLOWER WATCHING

IT WAS THE YEAR of our tenth anniversary when Antoine and I separated. I stayed in the house and he occupied a loft in Old Montreal, an outdatedly slick place with a rain shower and an ostentatious spiral staircase that ascended into a bedroom by way of a round opening barely wider than shoulder width. In better times, Antoine's advertising agency had used this condo to put up art directors and executives when they came to Montreal for longer stretches. One could imagine them, Germans in zippered black sweaters, muttering mantras on form following function while trying to get their suitcases to the second floor.

I visited him there after a few months. His bags were messily half full in the corner of the living room and there was an extra-large pizza box in the fridge with a fork and knife left in for repeated use. Cutlery in the pizza box had been a mainstay during Antoine's university years. Now I wondered whether it was a live habit that he'd been suppressing throughout our marriage.

"I am waiting for you to figure your shit out," he said.

He was waiting. Like a person waits for a bus, he was waiting, safe in the knowledge that, tick-tock, soon enough, the bus will arrive.

It was children he wanted.

He would say it and I would get an empty-bowlish feeling in my gut, a rolling echo, a valley of *not yet*.

"And what do you have going on, anyway?" he asked.

I had an idea that, with Antoine gone, other things would expand. I had a book that had built itself up in my mind as being some kind of portal. But now I'd spend mornings raking through the first drafts of first chapters, looking for a live coal, and every paragraph trailed into ash. I'd brush myself off midsentence to online-shop for vintage skirts and interesting things I might frame and put over the toilet. The doorbell rang and it would be another pencil skirt that didn't fit properly, another precious print that was clearly a photocopy. But I told Antoine that my boredom, my non-starting, felt somehow gravid. Like if I held on, something would manifest.

Antoine said it was all about becoming a mother, those feelings. *Something will manifest?* What else could it be? *Gravid?*

Even the most uninterested strangers can get the breeze off the childless thirty-eight-year-old woman's biological pendulum; time like a wagging finger, on this side, a life, on the other, some curdling mystery.

It's hard not to be swayed by this kind of consensus.

When Antoine moved back in, his shoulders were squared with a sense of mission. We had come to an agreement: fruition. We engaged in the necessary sex—one day on, one day off, to give the lifebloods a chance to regenerate. On weekends, we visited friends with babies as a retrenching activity, folding our legs on play mats studded with crazy talking cows and chunky wooden puzzle pieces. I was okay on these outings, sometimes even fizzing, elated—there were people with young children. Skies did not fall—but on the way home I would feel a gathering in my chest. I'd make Antoine stop for wine, for twelve-dollar fashion magazines, for cigarettes, having become all welled up with newly urgent ideas, sharply possible in the instant of their conjuring:

"You know, I've never been to Berlin. I've heard amazing things about those house-trade sites. You can do months, full seasons. Or what about Barcelona?"

MY GYNECOLOGIST HAD some mild reservations about my uterus, which she described as "hanging back." Antoine and I were soon visiting a fertility clinic, just in case. The clinic was in the old, decrepit English hospital on Mont Royal, a sharply turreted Victorian pile that looked like the hell side of universal medicine, this horned building. Manoir Frankenstein, I called it, rolling my eyes back and sticking out my arms rigidly before me, until Antoine told me to stop. The questionnaire we were given at our first visit was like a surgeon's magnifying lamp unapologetically aimed. *How long have you, as a couple, been trying to conceive?*

Two months? Two years? What does it mean, *trying?*

"Any birth control in that time?" asked the doctor.

I should have been glad we'd landed this doctor, hand patting, but still in ownership of a sense of duty. He wore a coercively cheery chick-yellow tie with tiny green trees on it. If you squinted, it looked like a herb omelet had flown onto his shirtfront, care of Hermès.

"No birth control? Never?"

Sometimes, during more beastly arguments, I said to Antoine that we were at the clinic for a failing sex life — offering up our flattened, tracked-on desire as a medical issue. But the doctor soon found that only one percent of Antoine's sperm were moving.

When Antoine heard this, he turned to me and said, *See?*

The doctor told Antoine that acupuncture might be marginally effective. A urologist could loosen some knotted veins in the testes, which sometimes helped in some minor way.

"But anything we do to Monsieur is just caressing the issue, playing nice. If you don't want to lose time, then we should just find the few most active sperm in Monsieur's sample, and do everything through Madame by in vitro fertilization. Statistically, this is by far the strongest option."

The doctor had photos of his children in carefully chosen frames on the dark bookcase beyond his desk. His children looked Asian, and, given the doctor's whiteness, and his specialty, this made one extremely curious to know whether the mother was also Asian. Near the picture frames, there was a kid's handmade card, wax crayon pressed hard into construction paper, *Papa + Isa + Olivier + Maman = Amour.*

ANTOINE DIDN'T MAKE any acupuncture appointments. I bought him an array of supplements at the health food store, dark glass bottles from Switzerland with convincing names like Virili-Vie and Fertil-Or, and he said it was not the time for hocus-pocus. He repeated that it wasn't him who needed to start making appointments now, it was me. Statistics said.

It was at this point that Antoine's oldest friend, Vincent Lussier, began hanging around the house, heat-seeking. It was actually good timing. In Vincent, Antoine and I could locate some harmony, finding a bit of our better selves in the depths of Vincent's fresh, fascinating despair.

Somehow, Vincent Lussier had ended up twice divorced in a single year. The first split was from Laurence, his wife of ten years, an angular television broadcaster with whom he'd never had any children. We assumed she and Vincent hadn't wanted any, or that Laurence couldn't, both assumptions equally substantiated when, weeks into Vincent's new bachelorhood, he made a girl pregnant on a one-night stand, a young intern named Océane. During the pregnancy, Vincent moved into her condo. But the coupling felt put-on, cardboardish, and in her last trimester Océane left to live with her mother in Ottawa.

None of this was at all characteristic. Vincent wasn't like Antoine's other friends, the *bon chic*, magnum-ordering agency guys with bleeping cars. He had a quiet seriousness that Antoine sometimes mocked as pigeon-toed, prudish. Antoine's judgements had been hauled, unchanged, through his relationship with Vincent; a friendship that began in elementary school.

So it was hard to know what to do with the new material. Vincent was now subletting the furnished top floor of a creaking duplex in the students' ghetto on the other side of Mont Royal. He called it his apartment with "the bathtub in the living room." He would stand in our living room or in the kitchen, in some spot of sunlight, and silently examine things, as if of utmost interest, examples from the world of normal: anthropologist of plant in window; of daily inspirational quote memo pad:

What we call luck is merely inner man externalized. We make things happen to us. — *Robertson Davies*

"Do you like Robertson Davies, Vincent?"

"I don't know. Is he a politician?"

Vincent was a strategist for the Parti Québécois. He had been in advertising, at the same agency as Antoine, before, but made the switch because he said he wanted to work towards a cause other than soap flakes. Antoine framed his friend's move into politics as square, calling Vincent a man with a burden of outdated ideas. Who said soap flakes anymore?

Soon Vincent began coming over before Antoine was even home from work. He'd arrive, and it was irritating, but then I would relax into a charitable cheerfulness. There was relief in Vincent's plane of depression, where time was moving at an outcast's pace. I made big, silly iced coffees with instant powder and ice cream. We sometimes sat on the small painted balcony that opened off my office, reading our respective newspapers while kids played street hockey on the road. I told Vincent how the shimmering leaves of the stippled white birches lining the side of the house hid bats. You could never see them, sleeping in the daytime, only flying around the telephone wires at night.

Vincent said the trees were quaking aspens, not birches.

"People call them the weeds of the forest," said Vincent. "Because they will grow anywhere. They don't care about conditions. They just take root."

IN BED. ANTOINE told me that Vincent was going to his office at odd hours, to avoid co-workers. "You think so?" I asked, turning to put out the light, staying turned.

"I am sure. He said he doesn't trust himself around people right now. Like he's afraid he'll just fuck more people up."

I felt both flattered and jealous. Vincent didn't share any of that kind of information on our afternoons.

"It's actually pretty conceited," continued Antoine, pulling at the sheets. "Like what? *Vincent Lussier, Dark Force? Beware of my huge light sabre dick?*"

WHEN VINCENT'S SUBLET ran out, it seemed preordained that he would stay with us until he found another place. Before his arrival, I was surprised by how much I was looking forward to having him as a guest. I changed plain bathroom soaps to round ones that came in pleated tissue paper; I retrieved from the cabinet over the fridge the lacquer-red espresso machine that Antoine and I never used; I cleared Antoine's winter clothes out of the guest room closet, and did a triage of the remaining hangers, leaving only the various wood and velvet-covered ones, nicer, even if they all curved into each other inconveniently.

I signed up for a one-month trial subscription to the cheerless French nationalist newspaper that Vincent read so that we would have that paper in the morning too. On the morning it first came, Antoine thought it was a wrong delivery. I found it, still with its elastic, in the recycling box. Vincent arrived that afternoon. He was pulling a rolling bag, and holding a pot of cleanly furled white calla lilies for me. The paper was unrolled on his bed.

"Just in case you didn't read today's," I said, my face flushing with my many preparations.

I stayed in my office the rest of the afternoon, watching words repel each other, the white space leering between: *She ... said ... what ... nevertheless.* At five, I took a bottle of wine into the living room. The cork came out noisily. The August sun was gentle on the sofa cushions, beams of floating dust winking occasionally with passing birds.

Footsteps came down the stairs.

"Hey! I was expecting my ice cream coffee," said Vincent, taking pleasure in the familiarity. He was more animated than I had seen him in a while.

"You are undermining our sacred ritual!" he said, rubbing his hands together, ready for some wine. When Vincent and Antoine were in college together, Vincent was a nerd while Antoine was in some upper echelon of popularity and cokeish weekend intrigue. You could sometimes see remnants of their nineteen-year-old world.

A large picture book was open on my lap. Vincent asked for it, and began flipping hard.

"This book is extremely gorgeous," he said, brows knit. "*Extremely.*"

His overinvestment made me want to look at the sofa velvet instead of at him. I had the book for a freelance assignment that I'd taken only because there was nothing else on my plate. I was translating an article from French to English for a barely-read government-funded tourism magazine that ran every piece in both official languages, side by side, every page an eye-crossing Franco-Anglo washboard of six-point type. The article was about a Quebec photographer who went around shooting gardens at night. Her pictures from the Mont-real Botanical Gardens were collected into the book Vincent was still holding.

"Antoine said you'd have to be the worst photog-rapher on earth to fuck up a close-up of an orchid," I said. "Even in the dark."

Vincent answered that this sounded like Antoine.

He pointed to a photo of an iris, a periwinkle curve exploding from blackness.

"In Japan there is a highly developed art of flower watching," he said. "I think it's a Zen thing. They put a screen behind an iris and watch it unfold for hours."

Vincent was wearing unlikely shorts; silky, basket-ball shorts, the type of shorts that told me Vincent did not usually wear shorts. His knees were flat and round, little boy's knees. His feet were bare and white and with the sort of lumpy bunions I'd only seen on women before, after a couple of decades of high heels.

Earlier that afternoon, he'd left the house, a note on the landing, "out for my walk." Something about the "my" depressed me; Vincent trying to create normalcy out of thin air. Confident in my understanding of my home's various creaks and warnings, I left my office and went into the guest room after he'd left.

In his bathroom, a neat canvas toiletries bag with a soap-stained bottom was tightly zippered. I opened it and looked, first with only one eye. You can locate too much tender information in this kind of bag—the futile hopes in the tube of whitening toothpaste, the twitching neurosis in the EpiPen.

Vincent's toiletries were all very clean, as if he wiped everything after use. He had a small dropper bottle of essential oil called Boreal Relax. It smelled of sweet, stripped cedar branches, making me for a moment long for some snowbanked childhood season, school cancelled, my neck warmer metallic with frozen saliva. I imagined Vincent rubbing the oil into his temples before bed, hoping for easy transport into the next day. On his bedside table was a paperback called *Everything Falls Apart: Zen Stories for Hard Times*. He'd spent a lot of time underlining one particular passage:

> *The nun Chiyono studied for years but was unable to find enlightenment. One night, she was carrying an old pail filled with water. As she was walking along, she was watching the full moon reflected in the pail of water. Suddenly, the bamboo strips that held the pail together broke, and the pail fell apart. The water rushed out; the moon's reflection disappeared, and Chiyono became enlightened. She wrote this verse:*
>
> > *This way and that way I tried to keep the pail together,*
> >
> > *hoping the weak bamboo would never break.*
> >
> > *Suddenly the bottom fell out.*

*No more water, no more moon in the water — emptiness
in my hand.*

Vincent returned from his walk charged, breathless,
pulling earbuds out of his ears. I stood on the landing,
as if I had only then seen his note.

"I was just listening to this podcast," he said, taking
two stairs at a time, holding up a plucked earbud. "And
the guy in the podcast tells this story, and it's the exact
story I just read in a book. I just read it last night! Isn't
that incredible? Fucking universe, eh?"

I POURED VINCENT some wine and now asked him what
that story was. He told me the nun story, almost as if
memorized. I watched his mouth open and close. I was
saved from comment by the ringing telephone. It was
Antoine. He would be at work late.

"Are you okay with Vincent?"

"I'm fine."

"Is he being weird?"

"Yes."

"Okay. Well. Don't forget you have appointments in
the morning."

I hung up the phone.

"Antoine will be late?" asked Vincent, draining his
wineglass.

"Yup."

Vincent came and sat on the sofa. I was by then taking pills, large-dose vitamins and hormones that made me wonder if I smelled. Sometimes I felt like I had the odour of someone other than myself, like a straphanger in a Paris metro, or a person using a public toilet whose scent clings after they've left the lavatory. Two or three times a day, I showered. My pee had this syrupy smell of stale sugar cereal.

I was skipping periods. I had never skipped periods before. Some women in the fertility clinic waiting room, women who all seemed to be professional in vitro fertilization experts, women who came in with kept folders and colour-coded calendars, told me this was happening only because I was now watching. Across the waiting room, expert fertility patients nodded into their binders at this, as if the subtle feminine body, the *inside* body, functions best when you least pay attention.

Vincent caught my eyes and closed his lids for a moment, tipping his head and raising his empty glass in a small, kind, stately way that made me grow quiet, because it showed that Vincent understood that I felt foul. I'd never told him about the clinic, and I doubt Antoine would have. But maybe the house was osmoting information.

I excused myself, and went upstairs, to my bathroom,

wanting to put my nose into my T-shirt, to check the state of myself. The window in the bathroom was open. Just after Antoine had moved back in, a bat had flown in through this window. Antoine killed it with a tennis racquet. He put the bat, small as an egg with its wings folded, in a white plastic bag and left it on the balcony to throw out the next day. But the following morning, when Antoine went to retrieve it, it was gone.

Vincent was waiting for me outside the bathroom.

I said, "Oh, hi."

He said, "How about—," and then put his mouth on mine, its insides shocking velvet. He smelled of deodorant, a European smell, like powdery violets, like soap.

"I'm sorry, Vincent, I feel like I —"

"You feel fucking wonderful."

PAIN OPENS PORTALS; kismet feeds on messes. It's only when everything is going to pieces that you see the patterns—the precision laser messages in pop songs; the premonitions in diary entries. This is the magic of nothing to lose. So Antoine soon had to leave for two days in Chicago, and I mistook the clearing for the blessing of fate.

His first morning away, I knew better than to stay home spinning weird webs in my head. Vincent had also left the house early, and in a suit, some real-world wind flapping his jacket's side vents. I'd had an affair before, in my very early years with Antoine. I couldn't now remember the man's face well, and was superstitious to go online for it, because I could too easily summon images of myself in this house, the rooms still smelling of paint and wallpaper paste, waiting for calls or emails, evenings devolving into nights of extreme cutlery-drawer management and charged-cellphone palming. Too many times, no call would come. I would join Antoine in bed, my head barely touching the pillow so as not to squash my hair, some pathetic hope still alive in me, inextinguishable.

I went to the botanical gardens. I brought the book of photographed flowers. I'd see the blooms that had been photographed at night during the daytime, the most non-required research trip in the history of government-funded magazine-translation gigs, but still, ostensibly, work.

The Gardens looked to be between seasons even though it was high summer. Many of the leaves were brown, the hedges tired, the grasses patched with yellow. I thought either June and July had been too hot or the person co-ordinating the planting of this place got their cycles mixed up.

The city sun burned between the straps of my sandals. I walked towards the various indoor pavilions, Chinese, Japanese, First Nations, passing a rose briar where tanned gardeners in utility belts and T-shirts that read ETUDIANT were tying white bags with breathing holes onto bushes, working with swift, silent concentration. I imagined them having beers at the café outside the gift shop after work, all of them together, muscles aching satisfactorily. They were too young to have made many mistakes yet. I wanted to call out and ask why they were bagging the plants but was suddenly too shy to break their rhythm.

THE HOUSE WAS trapped with heat when I got home. The calla lilies Vincent brought me were drooping like some terrible metaphor. Newly attuned to plant life after my day at the Gardens, I took the pot into the bathtub, leaving it on the tub floor while I showered over it. I was drying off when Vincent came home, looking as determined as when he'd left in the morning. He knocked on the bathroom door and we landed in the tub, Vincent beneath me, more urgent this time. The plant pot was still there, and the back of Vincent's head kept meeting its earth, sending the scent of soil and leaf into the steamy bathroom.

I thought of how I'd once tried keeping flower petals in my bra all day so as to be specially scented for Antoine at night. It was a fanciful touch I'd read of in a novel, and too romantic for my household. When I undressed, Antoine looked up at my approaching body and said, *"Petite*, you have a leaf stuck on your boob."

Later that night, I told Vincent that story. He lay on my bed, refusing to get under the sheets. The night outside was an oddly bright, troutish colour. He'd asked if I could draw the curtains, and then complained he was too hot. Potting soil was crumbling onto his pillow. I laughed at this, our little bit of recent shared history, but he flinched when I raised my hand to brush some dirt off his hairline. He looked like he was in pain.

"Are you thirsty? I have been told I make an *excellent* instant coffee with ice cream," I chirped, cutely.

But Vincent said it was clearly too late for that sort of thing. And when I woke in the morning, it was to the sound of his leaving through the front door. I came out of the bedroom, and surveyed the carpet on the landing for a note. No note.

I knew for sure that Vincent was in his suit again, because it was not in his closet. Would he be back in the evening? Antoine was not due to return for another day yet. Instantly, I became stuck on the question of whether Vincent would be at home for dinner. The very idea of his not returning for dinner flourished into full female insult in my chest, even though I had nothing planned, even though it was just me, standing alone, on my landing, in my underwear. I could not phone him, at 9 a.m., to ask about supper. A quote, from some distantly recalled short story, rose through my synapses:

She had turned him into the peg on which her hopes were hung.

You can't make them back into a person once you've done that.

I couldn't think of anything to do but shop, cheery me with the clerks, wishing everyone a good, great day. Filets, foie gras, some overly expensive American Cabernet, which the label pretentiously named a claret.

Who said claret anymore? I would laugh, popping the cork.

I went into a lingerie store and looked at stockings with ribbons threaded elaborately through their tops. Agent Provocateur, read the tag. I remembered the daze of fancy panties and self-care I had years before entered into when the eyes of a man who was not my husband were expected all over me. Back then, even when it was idiotic, it never felt idiotic.

I came home and sat in front of my computer. I ate the foie gras on crackers and then felt bad for it, because sitting in front of my computer was no special occasion. I looked up flower watching online but found only web sites having to do with Japanese cherry blossom parties, these big, drunken commercial events in parks, the cherry trees blooming for just one springtime week, the cleanup taking twice as long.

I tried going onto Vincent's Facebook page but found that he'd disabled it, and, just as certainly, that this felt like a personal affront.

He did show up for dinner. I offered to do the filets in a pan, but he listlessly said he would get a pizza. He was out for nearly two hours and returned with the smallest pie. He said he'd assumed I would have fixed my meat or whatever by then, but he reddened at these words, because we could both see the truth, crueller than usual, that Vincent could only now cringe at the thought of giving me anything. As if he had already given me the world.

He soon left the house. He was organizing a Quebec delegation for a world francophone summit in Ottawa. While at the summit, he'd stay with Océane and her mother and their child. There, he would learn that his own parents had been making frequent trips to Ottawa, to see their grandchild. After the summit a dinner was organized—Vincent and Océane and the baby and the three grandparents, a whole family, ready-made.

I knew all this from Antoine. We sat in the waiting room of the fertility clinic and he told me these things, taking my silence for nervousness. Antoine kept on drawing unusable samples. The idea of a donor had been mentioned by the doctor. The results on his desk were never good, but on this day the results on his desk would be different. The child's card was gone, but I remembered it: *Papa + Isa + Olivier + Maman = Amour.*

"Madame is pregnant," said the doctor. "I would say about a month in."

It didn't take long for either Antoine or me to complete the math. We sat in a dumpling place near the hospital, our mouths dry, our world tipped sideways. Vincent would return for a discussion, we agreed. We would not discuss anything until Vincent returned for a discussion. Before Vincent returned for the discussion, a small white sac disappeared down a red toilet bowl.

ABOUT A YEAR later, one of the babies Antoine and I had visited just after he'd moved back in came over with her mother. The girl was now nearly three, giving the performance of a song she'd learned at daycare. My house felt too still in her presence, and I wondered if, singing in my living room, she could sense it. She toddled, mid-tune, to a low bookshelf and pulled out the book of the flowers at night.

She opened the book and began scratching at a page.

"*Chérie*," said her mother, "*c'est pas un* scratch and sniff, *ça.*"

"*Mais, Maman*," said the child. "In this book, I can smell the flowers!"

"*Ah, oui?*"

"*Oui, Maman*, and I can hear them speaking too —"

"*Une fleur qui parle?*"

"*Oui, Maman,* these flowers here are saying they would like a puppy!"

"*Un puppy?*"

"Yes, they want one because they are sad. They are in the dark, and nobody can see them! Do you see the way nobody can see them, *Maman?*"

ESKIMOS

GERRY DUBINSKY WAS STANDING outside his house, shovelling snow banked as high as his hips, when his keys fell out of his pocket. The snow was new and expanding, and swallowed the keys so completely he couldn't even find the pit where they'd hit the surface. Gerry looked across the road. It was two days before the new year, only two degrees below zero, but the dampness made it feel colder. The houses on Lexington Crescent were dark, the street decamped to its dopplegäng of Florida condos—Casa Goldberg, Manoir Altman. Gerry peered again at the ground. Heavier, bluish flakes had begun falling, flakes with water in them, and now little pits were appearing everywhere in the snow, which was just as bad for key-finding: first no sign and now hundreds of maybes.

It was Saturday. He was wearing flannel pyjama bottoms that Lori bought him that said PEEJAYS across the ass. Lori had a thing for buying stuff that told you what it was: the pump soap in the bottle that said SOAP; the mugs ringed COFFEE&TEA&COFFEE&TEA. Their house once had a 97 painted black in the glass half moon over the front door, and Lori got it scraped off and instead had this platter-sized piece of slate drilled into the house's facade, which read NINETY-SEVEN LEXINGTON CRESCENT, all written out, even the number. It looked like a memorial plate, or one of those heritage plaques you'd see on old buildings in Europe. *Here lived Charles Dickens. Here lived Moishe Pupick. Here lived Gerry Dubinsky (b. 1955, d. 2014), restaurateur, who froze to death in idiotic pyjama pants while his wife Lori Schacter (b. 1968) was in Santa Barbara, getting her face fixed.*

Getting it fixed more. Further fixed. Gerry hoped his ski jacket covered the PEEJAYS. He dug his shovel into the snow and began walking to Levin's, Levin Wiseman, his oldest friend, the traditional safe house for Gerry's spare keys.

The last time Gerry was at Levin's, he was dropping off Lori's latest garbage bags of clothes for the Wiseman cleaning lady to send to her village near Manila.

Levin's wife, Ruth — who was also Gerry's first wife — had come to the glass-fronted door with disbelieving eyes.

"*More?*" she mouthed, unlocking.

"Meet my wife," said Gerry, dragging bags up the front steps.

With Lori there were bags every month. She said she was just "being a super-generous person," but her rabid impatience in getting her cast offs out of the house after she'd decided against things pointed to weirder, less magnanimous motives.

"Our maid stopped taking anything," Gerry said, sliding the bags onto the squeaky hallway floorboards. Ruth was still in her bathrobe. She was holding one of those old-style accordion blowers for a fireplace. The house smelled pleasantly of pancakes, or something with maple syrup.

"She saw the price tag still on a pink silk thing," continued Gerry, wanting Ruth to know this story. "I think it was a windbreaker, Lori was throwing it out like a piece of garbage, and the maid got superstitious, because this glorified hankie was the price of two years of tuition in the Philippines —"

Ruth laughed. "You know, I've been raiding the bags for the twins," she said, her two girls away at Queen's. "The less insanely sexy stuff —"

Gerry told Ruth her secret was safe. With Lori, he kept his mouth shut about these things. He liked the good life as much as anyone, but he was pretty sure a three-thousand-dollar windbreaker should not exist;

that a three-thousand-dollar windbreaker could, cat-
egorically, only be a bad thing. If he piped up, Lori
would say it was her money. She would tell him not to
be like his father.

*Here lived Gerry Dubinsky (b. 1955, d. 2014), son of Sid-
ney Dubinsky (b. 1915, d. 2014), a man who had purchased
his own headstone in advance, twenty years before his death,
possibly because he'd found a sale somewhere, or some other
depressing reason.*

Sometimes Gerry wondered whether his father,
who died in April, hadn't meant to expire back when
he bought his grave marker. Maybe he had hoped the
acquisition of a headstone would expedite getting to lie
under it. It was around the time of the purchase that
Mr. Dubinsky stopped speaking, one morning, a complete mute by some internal imperative nobody tried
too hard to crack. In the case of Sid Dubinsky's voice,
the question of what was lost was a hard one for Gerry
to answer.

And so it was for his death. There are people who
just add zero to the world, so fully impermeable are
they in their skin, that barely anything goes in or out.

On the second and last day of Mr. Dubinsky's
truncated two-day shiva, nobody but Ruth and Levin
showed up. When Gerry's rabbi arrived, Levin had to
go knocking door to door to find the necessary ten for
a prayer quorum.

Levin's father, the labour leader, passed away a month later and a thousand people came to the funeral. The shiva was an eight-day riot of fresh tears and overlapping deli platters. Ruth saw poor Gerry, standing by the Danish pastries, making comparisons on the sidelines of what she'd named "Levin's grieving ball."

"Remember, Gerry," she said, "a blowhard who speaks softly is just a covert blowhard. Levin's family love nothing better than to get together and tell each other how righteous they are. The mission isn't to make everyone else feel morally decrepit. It's just the effect."

THE SNOW WAS coming down harder, caking in the creases of Gerry's ski jacket, releasing in chunks as he trundled over plow-made mountains. He pushed back his sleeve to look at his watch. Levin was doing a full year of Kaddish for his father, saying prayers at synagogue every single morning, but it was ten and Gerry guessed he'd be home by now. Maybe Ruth would have pancakes waiting.

Ruth first met Gerry's dad in the 1970s — a meal was convened at the nasty Polish place Sid Dubinsky ate at three times a week anyway. Ruth was a student at the university's music conservatory. Her parents owned a luncheonette near campus, and Gerry worked there to fund his B.A. He and Ruth had just become engaged. After a nearly silent dinner, Gerry's father shovelling his stew with a fork held like an ice pick, the bill arrived — the goulash seventy-five cents a portion; the price of tea, fifteen cents — and Mr. Dubinsky looked at his son and then at Ruth, and asked frankly if they expected him to pay for their food.

After only three years of marriage, Gerry and Ruth divorced. The split happened when Gerry was opening his first restaurant — a small place, but with a bar licence. He was deal-making with the type of people you have to know to break into the restaurant business, and found himself ashamed when introducing his plain-faced wife to investors. Here was Ruth, with her little eyes like black marbles and her sturdy ankles and threadbare Chinese flats and fingers raw from too much piano. Every night she would lie on the bedroom carpet for what seemed like hours to do her posture work, and if Gerry made a joke and lay on top of her, her outrage was such that he felt like a criminal trying to get into a nun's panties.

But now that Ruth is a well-known pianist, Gerry understands that he should have had more patience. He also thinks that maybe Lori — who is like a force field of hyperactivity, a pressure system of pins and needles that expands to fill every empty space with static — was payback for his mistakes with Ruth.

His second wife, Sharna, always said Gerry was, in his true nature, a floater, not grounded enough to be happily married to anyone. This was rich coming from flaky Sharna, with her acupuncturists and palm readers, but still he knew what she meant. In Gerry's heyday, when he owned a dozen restaurants up and down the Main, he kept a nameplated booth at every one of them. He would sit at those tables and know where to find his feet. But now he seemed to be missing some essential sense everyone else had. In his own home, he often felt like a person doing a pantomime of his own life: *and now I will blow out these birthday candles thoughtfully placed by my wife; and now I will relax and read the newspaper in bed, for it is Sunday morning.*

Sharna used to say Gerry had existential issues because he was without tethering background or culture, because he had no mother and his father was a miser, a son of a bitch, and a communist.

"My father was barely a communist," Gerry pointed out. "He wasn't dedicated to that at all."

"Even worse," said Sharna. "So you have a big hole where your meaning should go and not a thing to fill it with, not even communism."

In his whole life, Gerry never belonged to a synagogue. Lori didn't belong because she said she was an atheist. When Gerry needed a rabbi to bury his father, Lori sent him to the Reform because it was the closest place to their house.

The Reform rabbi was new, a lesbian with a wife and two kids. In her office, beyond the temple's pathologically sunlit chapel, she wore a crappy pinstriped suit, like a twelve-year-old Orthodox boy missing his sidelocks. Gerry has no recollection of her saying anything about a year of Kaddish. At the end of their meeting to discuss his father's funeral, she gave him a book with three stacked rocks on the cover, *Mindfulness for Grief*. They weren't rocks stacked in the shape of a man, like those piles granola-types loved making on camping trips, just three smooth stones, the kind masseuses heated up and put on your back.

"You might find this book helpful," said the rabbi, pushing it across the table.

"Is this a Reform book?"

"No. It's pretty generic, and by that I mean universal. You can keep it."

Here lived Gerry Dubinsky, who probably missed half the shit he was supposed to do after his father's death because all he could think about near his lesbian rabbi was how she was intimate with her wife, like the real logistical questions in it, like, was there a top person and a bottom person? And if you were a rabbi, did that mean you were automatically on top? And was it just rubbing, or was there use of something that went inside?

LEVIN AND RUTH'S could be reached by shortcut, a staircase that ran down from a lookout at the southernmost point of Lexington Crescent. People called the steps the Real Estate Ladder because at the top of them, you could add a few million to your house price. Gerry surveyed the staircase, heaped with snow, and saw that the only way he could make it down would be if he slid on his rear.

This is the point in the Canadian winter, Gerry thought to himself, where the only place the weather makes total sense is on a ski hill. Gerry hadn't even had his skis serviced that year. He reimagined his day: driving up to Mont Tremblant; attacking the black diamond runs right off the bat; the evergreens at the summit dripping with icicles; the skiers all in it together. Gerry would eat extra-large lumberjack orders of poutine and sugar pie for lunch, satisfied with the feeling of having earned his meal.

He now turned to look back at the curving street, to see whether anyone was around. Barely a house was left on Lexington where the old brick hadn't been refaced with stone. The exteriors all looked weirdly the same now, smooth, grey, tablet-like, Lexington Crescent like the dentures of God, a half moon of giant, matching tombstones. Lori recently modernized their own house, replacing the back porch where Gerry smoked his cigars with a glass cube of a sunroom Lori called the

Library. White lacquered floor-to-ceiling shelves were filled with colour-matched books a decorator bought by the foot. There were bird guides next to textbooks in French next to old novels nobody's ever heard of, all in service of lilac-to-grape.

With his porch gone, the only place in the house left for Gerry alone was the basement sauna and its adjoining bathroom, which so far flew under Lori's renovation radar, remaining the same as when they first bought the house. The walls were cedar, the bathroom hardware and sauna knobs rusted and ugly. Lori said the rooms were mouldy, but Gerry, who used the sauna all the time, liked them. The diagonal wood slats looked alpine to him, and he nailed a pair of his old Kneissls, criss-crossed, over the toilet, along with a few photos from ski hills, sunny pictures from the pre-Lori days, Gerry in his mirrored goggles and orange Lange boots with those tight ski pants that belled over them.

Here lived Gerry Dubinsky, who was found dead in his sauna, waiting for his Viagra to come on so that he could successfully enter his wife Lori, who wanted it every single night, and sometimes in the morning too, and sometimes Gerry would wake up at 2 a.m. and his spouse would be humping him like an animal, and sometimes she wanted Gerry to pee on her, and sometimes she wanted Gerry to pee inside her, and Gerry would feel the walls closing in, like the walls of his house were Lori's flesh made wall, and only if he got outside could he breathe. Neighbours who saw the automatic lights over the front door go on at 3 a.m. suspected that Dubinsky was just smoking too much.

AT THE TOP of the snow-piled Real Estate Ladder, Gerry considered the options: soaked pyjamas and shorter distance to Levin and Ruth's, or longer distance and dryer bottoms. He wasn't wearing underwear, which now seemed an issue. Snow had already pocketed into the back of his boots, creating a growing circle of wet on his calves. It was a familiar feeling. He was relieved when he identified it as a childish feeling: wet pyjama. He looked down at his boots. They looked like shit-brown oven mitts on his feet. Lori bought them for him, as if he were just another Zoe or Chloe, clomping around the neighbourhood in sweatpants with words on the rear.

Here lived Gerry Dubinsky, at one time known as King of the Main, who fell to his death trying to slide down the Real Estate Ladder while dressed like a teenaged girl —

At Levin's father's shiva, Ruth said she had a hard time believing that Gerry's rented rabbi would have *forgotten* to tell him about Kaddish.

"Nobody would have expected you to do a Saint Levin and draw it out for the year," she said. "But she must have offered some option, even just to try to get you to join the synagogue —"

Gerry said he guessed it was possible she'd said something. He hadn't been able to concentrate.

"The lesbian thing?"

"No."

"Right."

In truth, Gerry was surprised at how completely his rabbi's sexual orientation had coated his brain. He'd seen things, in his day. Once, two of his waitresses made out for him behind the bar on New Year's Eve, and Gerry later took them into the bathroom with some coke. Still, that was more girl-on-girl action; it wasn't the real thing. He'd never known a woman who felt like a man, or wanted to be manly, or whatever it was lesbians felt. For days after his first meeting with the rabbi, Gerry puzzled over what it would take to convert a true lesbian. Even for one night. A big dick would not do it. That might even be a turnoff. It would have to happen through the mind. The rabbi would have to fall in love with Gerry's insides, enough to over-look the shell of him.

Gerry told Ruth how the rabbi had a psychology degree hanging on her office wall, near her rabbinical degree.

"So I asked her about it, and she said, 'Remember how they used to say psychology is the new religion? Well, the opposite is true again.' She couldn't make a living as a shrink, so she said she went back to school when she was forty and became a rabbi."

"Uplifting," said Ruth, dryly. "Although maybe she missed the class on mourning."

But Gerry actually did find the rabbi's career change inspiring. He liked the practicality: *oh well, I guess I'll become a rabbi.* Certainly, the rabbi didn't look to have some outsized confidence or capability. She was a small person, with a small chin and a quivering kid's voice. Her brown hair was so light that her bangs flapped up when she dropped herself into her leather desk chair. Gerry could sometimes be mysteriously attracted to not very good-looking people, but this rabbi was next-level interesting because she wasn't even *trying.* Maybe she was even doing the opposite, like guys on the news who dye their hair grey to look more credible.

At the end of their meeting, the rabbi looked Gerry in the eyes and asked him if there was anything he wanted to share with her, since there would be no eulogies at Mr. Dubinsky's funeral.

"About my father?"

"Or about how you are feeling. Your only parent has expired."

"I have these little zings," Gerry said, finally, experimentally.

"What do you mean, zings?" said the rabbi, leaning forward.

"Like, I'll be doing something, and this picture will come up, of my dad, almost like a postcard."

He expected the rabbi to ask for an example, and he had one ready. He was a boy of eight, maybe nine, in that old neighbourhood of duplexes with black metal balconies and cracked-open windows exuding the smell of fried meat. It was the coldest day of the year, gristle-grey, with old snow mixed with salt and sand banking the sidewalks like huge pushed-aside portions of oatmeal. His father locked his house keys in the car and, even though right outside their duplex, he refused to ask any neighbours for help. He instead walked to a phone booth, and then waited with Gerry for CAA to come — this unshaven, walrus-faced man in sealskin galoshes and triangular Cossack hat, leaning against a dirty car, his mean, unopened suitcase of a life everything to strive against.

But the rabbi didn't ask for elucidation.

"Oh, those flash memories are normal," she waved. "I call them paradoxical light bulb moments. It's like an aha moment, you know, when the light bulb goes on over your head? Except after a loved one like your dear father dies, it's more like a light goes *off*."

The rabbi sat back in her chair. "Let's just let that idea settle," she said, breathing in for effect, crossing her arms over her chest, her bony wrists thin in her suit's too-large sleeves. Hers was a different kind of slimness from Lori's highly engineered, careerlike version, where veins ran thick and pulsing around so many firm island-mounds deposited by plastic surgeons or gym trainers. Maybe it was because Gerry's view was too close-range, but it was hard to tell with Lori, these days, if it was the look of effort, the aura of upkeep, that was so impressive, rather than the real physical outcome of the work. After all, half the attraction of fake tits is that you know the owner submitted to big surgery for *tits*.

The rabbi began talking again.

"So, what I think of as the classic paradoxical light bulb is, like, this moment, you know, where you're in the middle of your regular monologue, *First I am going to make those phone calls, then I have to go to the post office, then I have to return those videos, and then I will go see Dad about his—oh, no*...What you are getting, Gerry, is a variation."

When Gerry told Lori about this, later that afternoon, she said, "Video store? Post office? What are we? In the 1990s? Or in the Victorian times?"

Gerry wasn't sure the rabbi's theory applied, either. He was pretty sure he didn't miss his father. It was not surprising, but it was disappointing. He'd hoped for some more noble feelings. Ruth always said that Gerry would have had an easier time if his father had been a Holocaust survivor. At least then there would have been a good explanation for all of Sid Dubinsky's egregious lacks and absences.

The only time he'd ever set foot in any of Gerry's restaurants (he always said they were too far downtown or filled with "Mafia types") was for the wedding to Lori. The reception was at Gerry's most impressive place, the one with the golden, twenty-five-foot ceilings, yellow leather chairs, billowing white curtains, and glass columns that weighed a ton each. That place had a Michelin star. The menu was so premium that the restaurant needed seventeen grand a day in sales just to break even.

Gerry's father spent most of the dinner in the kitchen, where a small TV parked by the door on a busboy trolley had a playoff game on. Gerry came in to see the chef and found his father sitting, watching hockey, hunched over a plate of noodles instead of the truffled duck towers that were then being served. When, a couple of years later, Gerry's restaurants closed one after the other, from problems with investors, and then with the police because of his connections to those investors, and then with just being on the wrong side of fashion, his father said, "Good thing you married rich," and nothing else.

Gerry never imagined that his father could become dependent, that his tight-fisted self-sufficiency would ever collapse. And yet, in his father's last years, Gerry had to care for him. Even a full-service assisted living facility needs someone to call when a resident is sick, or has doctor's appointments, or mail from the government. At the very least, every week Gerry brought cash to the extra caregiver, a thin Jamaican with a prominent crucifix who said that even though the mute Mr. Dubinsky could growl at her like a street dog, she still felt humanity in his gaze. She bought him his clothes. Usually Gerry entered his father's quarters to find him sleeping in his wheelchair, a shrunken old man wearing an extra-large track suit emblazoned BOSS across the chest.

GERRY TESTED THE deep snow on the Real Estate Ladder to see how it would react to his weight. He dipped one of his brown oven-mitt boots in and his foot came out without the boot. This was glutinous snow; the kind of snow that cemented into your ski bindings. If you fell, your skis would twist your kneecap off before releasing. Still: stupid boots.

Here lived Gerry Dubinsky, who in his fifties became a hundred percent financially dependent on his third wife, Lori Schacter, only child of strip mall magnate Sol Schacter, a patriarch who possibly did not know the extent of his daughter's mental issues. Dubinsky often asked himself whether Schacter had ever found his daughter, as Dubinsky had, crouched in a bathroom at midnight, desperately squeezing bottles of shampoo and lotion down the drain, in a litter of

already empty bottles, the ongoing action explained with:
"Stop staring at me, you fat fuck. Nothing here was more
than a quarter full." At first, Dubinsky attributed some of
his wife's behaviours to medication, but as his marriage pro-
gressed, he understood that the prescriptions made no dif-
ference, that Lori Schacter's system just burned pills up, the
drugs like tiny single drops of moisture on a hard-parched,
bone-dry desert floor.

On the second and final day of his father's under-
populated shiva, while waiting in the living room for
Levin to come back from canvassing neighbours for the
prayer quorum, Ruth asked Gerry whether he remembered the way her parents used to call Jews Eskimos.

Gerry shook his head. Ruth's parents were Irish
Jews, thickly accented, and at first not thrilled that their
gifted daughter was taking up with their luncheonette
waiter, when at the university there were med students
and budding lawyers to be had.

"Eskimos," repeated Ruth. "They would stand
behind the counter, scanning the place to scope out if
any other Jews were in the room."

"Why Eskimos?" asked Lori, who was sitting on a
sofa opposite Ruth, staring into her phone.

"They just wouldn't say Jew in public," said Ruth,
looking at Lori anyway.

"And they liked joking," added Gerry, diplomatically.

"Oh, for sure," agreed Ruth. "Table six is an igloo.

Table two wants to know how fresh the whale is. It was a convivial shame. It's funny to think about now."

"Well, I don't think it's funny," said Lori, now tapping at her phone screen. "I think it's really depressing. They could have at least said Member of the Tribe or Bagel-Eater. And isn't 'Eskimos' racist? Oh my god! I am so fed up with my phone. I am totally going to get a new one tomorrow."

Gerry searched out Ruth's eyes. What did he want? Sympathy?

"I better go through my pictures now," Lori continued, standing. "We don't want anyone at the phone store seeing anything they shouldn't be seeing, right, Ger?"

Levin returned with several men Gerry didn't know; Jonathan Altman's Torah study group. Altman, a hundred percent shmatte to the core, had some kind of spiritual rebirth after getting his thyroid taken out last year.

"I am sorry for your loss," said Altman to Gerry. Altman then waved at the lesbian rabbi, who had emerged from the kitchen and was passing around prayer books.

"Hiya, Rina," he said, and then turned to Gerry. "I didn't know you were at the Reform, Gerry. I don't think I've ever seen you there."

During the prayers, the rabbi rocked back and forth, her suit jacket flapping. Some of Altman's men loudly hummed the silent passages with their eyes shut, as if they might really send Gerry's father to heaven through the power of prayer. Lori nudged Gerry.

"I think I should delete this one," she mouthed, eyes doll-wide. She was holding up her phone screen, showing a photo of herself with a belt around her neck like a leash, and Gerry's hairy stomach, his big wink of a belly button, filling out the background.

Gerry went into the basement right after the prayers. He stood in the bathroom by his sauna, everything ridiculous, his lopsided ski pictures, his criss-crossed Kneissls, the diagonal wooden slats. His throat was as narrow as a stir stick. He opened the medicine chest and reached past a small wall of Viagra for the Ativan that he hid from Lori, and had a sudden image: how Lori was going to come at him that night, with this too-focused look, like she was sweating from her eyes. He shook his head, as if to change the channel, and saw himself going down on the lesbian rabbi. He heard Ruth and Levin saying goodbye to Lori upstairs. He imagined leaving with them, sleeping in one of their twins' empty bedrooms, waking up to Ruth still in her bathrobe, sitting at her piano, her low, wide hips and thick thighs comfortably spread across the bench, the skirt of her robe coming apart just a little.

"Any Eskimos around here?" he'd ask.

"No, just *eejits*," she'd giggle, using more of her parents' slang, turning towards him.

He once asked Lori what kind of sex life she thought Ruth and Levin had. Lori said Levin was like a man with no penis.

"Trust me, Ruth has cobwebs," she said. "Ruth is *dying* on the inside."

A FEW DAYS after his father's shiva, Gerry went to the rabbi's office to return some of the prayer books she'd left in the house. He decided he was going to really talk to her, use her like one was meant to use a rabbi, for guidance. He thought of that rag man Jonathan Altman and his easy familiarity: *Hiya, Rina.* He'd read pages of *Mindfulness for Grief*, trying to narrow his brain to the words, as if studying for an exam: *When grief is dealt with unskilfully, if it is repressed, it can initiate a chain of complications such as social withdrawal, panic attacks, and inappropriate responses to old memories.*

I think I am repressing, he would say to the rabbi. I think my responses are inappropriate. He would tell her how his father had been so turned in, so hard-hearted, the only excuse could have been the Holocaust, and the Holocaust was an excuse his father didn't have.

In her office, the rabbi was going through books on her shelves, examining the insides of covers, filling an open cardboard box on her desk.

"Skipping town?" asked Gerry.

"No," said the rabbi, shutting a book decisively and looking up. "But my wife is. She's going back to New York."

"Oh."

"I plan on being open about it with my congregation," said the rabbi, her voice so high it nearly whistled. "My policy is openness. We are a sharing community. It's a divorce."

Gerry stood with the prayer books.

"I'm sorry," he said.

"She had a good client base before we moved here. But she would have needed to retake part of her degree to practise in this province."

"What does she do?"

"She's a psychologist. I guess you don't go from being a big-shot Manhattan shrink to a Montreal student and stay-at-home mom, right? Are you returning those books?"

"I am," said Gerry, not knowing how to get to where he wanted now, talking to the rabbi.

"I know about divorce," he offered.

"Yes," said the rabbi. "Well, I wish you the best on your grief journey, Gerry. I hope I have helped you. I'd say see you soon, but your wife already told me you guys weren't interested in joining the synagogue."

WIND WAS GUSTING tiny tornadoes of snow along the surface of the stairs as Gerry prepared for his descent. He was going to slide down. He had a clear memory of an old television commercial, a cowboy waves his hat as he skids along a rainbow into a pot of lotto gold. Gerry took off his ski jacket and tied it around his waist, figuring that if he held the sides of the garment up against his outer thighs as he slid, he could keep his seat dry. The snow crunched as Gerry sat down, arranging himself. Close on the horizon, he could see his friends' house. Ruth's old Honda was in the driveway, Levin's SUV was not there. Gerry Dubinsky leaned forward, for that minute a man with a plan.

ACKNOWLEDGEMENTS

The people who gave me the earliest support after reading the first story in this collection have a special place in my heart: Ira Silverberg; Sarmishta Subramanian. David Rakoff (z"l), I will never forget your words of encouragement. Thanks as well to Ruth Curry, Alana Klein, and Jonathan Goldstein. Dr. Bahram Mokri at the Mayo Clinic, and Dr. Xiaoyang Liu in Montreal, I thank you. I am grateful and so happy for my agent, Anna Stein, and feel very indebted to Noah Richler and Jared Bland, who directed me to Sarah MacLachlan at Anansi, and to Sarah, for putting me in the hands of editor Janice Zawerbny.

The Handels, the Silcoffs, the Kronishes—thank you for everything. My husband, Michael, thank you.

I am so very grateful to the arts funding available in my country and province: to the Canada Council for the Arts, Le Conseil des Arts et des Lettres du Québec, and also to the Writers' Trust of Canada Woodcock Fund — the most generous grant, because it provides immediate support to authors facing difficult circumstances while writing. The Woodcock has helped save a lot of books, including this one.

© Sabrina Reeves

MIREILLE SILCOFF is the founding editor of *Guilt & Pleasure Quarterly*, a magazine of new Jewish writing and ideas, and is the author of three books about drug and youth culture. She is a lead columnist with Canada's *National Post* and a frequent contributor to the *New York Times Magazine* and other publications. She lives in Montreal.